Define
"Normal"

Define "Normal"

A NOVEL BY

JULIE ANNE PETERS

Little, Brown and Company
Boston New York London

First Paperback Edition

Library of Congress Cataloging-in-Publication Data

Peters, Julie Anne.
Define "normal" / by Julie Anne Peters — 1st ed.
p. cm.
Summary: When she agrees to meet with Jasmine as a peer counselor at their middle school, Antonia never dreams that this girl with the black lipstick and pierced eyebrow will end up helping her deal with the serious problems she faces at home and become a good friend.

ISBN 0-316-16233-7 (scholastic)
ISBN 0-316-73489-6 (pb)
ISBN 0-316-70631-0 (hc)

[1. Family problems — Fiction. 2. Friendship — Fiction. 3. Peer counseling — Fiction. 4. Parent and child — Fiction.] I. Title.

PZ7.P44158 De 2000
[Fic] — dc21 99-042774

HC: 10 9 8 7 6 5 4 3 2
PB: 10 9 8 7 6 5 4 3 2 1

MV-NY

Printed in the United States of America

To my brother John,
a legend in his own time

With thanks to my fine editor, Megan Tingley,
who makes me a better writer than I am

Define "Normal"

Chapter 1

I opened the door and froze. Not Jazz Luther. Couldn't be. Impossible. My jaw stuck in the gape-open position.

"What are you looking at?" Jazz sneered at me.

Your purple hair? Your black lips? Your shredded jeans? "Nothing," I muttered.

"You my peer counselor?" Jazz asked, clunking ankle-high boots up onto the conference table. She tipped back the chair and threaded her fingers together behind her head.

My stomach knotted. "Guess so." I thought, Define "peer."

Jazz snorted. She must've had the same thought.

Exhaling a long breath, I slid into a chair at the opposite end of the table. Even that far away, her perfume was noxious. Maybe it wasn't perfume. More like incense. The odor, a mix of musky and sweet, made my nose pucker. I smoothed down my pleated skirt, trying desperately not to sneeze. Or gag. "Where's Dr. DiLeo?" I asked.

"He had some emergency," she answered. "Probably ran out of Tic Tacs and had to rush over to 7-Eleven."

I stifled a laugh. Our school psychologist did reek of peppermint.

"So, you want to start or you want me to?" She leaned back farther in the chair, her boots scraping across the Formica tabletop. They left a noticeable black mark. Maybe the faculty conference room wasn't the ideal place to hold counseling sessions.

Start. Where to start? When Dr. DiLeo proposed the peer counseling program at Oberon Middle School, I'm sure he didn't think someone like Jazz Luther would sign up. No doubt he meant it for people with minor problems. Problems such as dealing with difficult teachers or getting bogged down with homework. Problems with boyfriends or jealous girlfriends. I don't know. Not someone with Jazz Luther's problems. She was hopeless. A punker. A druggie. A gang hanger. Peer counseling? Jazz needed long-term professional psychotherapy. "In a lock-up facility," I mumbled.

"Huh?" she said.

"Nothing. Why don't you go ahead." This should be good. "Tell me why you're here." Dr. DiLeo suggested the line as an icebreaker, a way to open a conversation. Although between us, there loomed an iceberg.

Jazz smirked. "It keeps me off the streets."

I forced a smile back. Good reason.

She flung her feet to the floor and stood. Her chair crashed into the metal heater behind her, leaving a dent. "Oops." She shrugged. Without picking up the chair, she clomped across the room toward me. "I can't talk to you clear down there." She yanked out a chair catty-corner to me and looped her left leg over the back. "I'm here because DiLeo says I gotta be. I gotta do fifteen hours of counseling this term." She slid the sleeve of her lavender leather jacket up an inch and glanced at her watch. "Ten minutes and counting." She grinned.

I couldn't get over how white her teeth looked against the black lipstick. Or maybe what distracted me was the earring in her eyebrow. "Doesn't that hurt?"

"What?" She frowned.

I touched my eyebrow.

"Naw. I mean, it hurt at first. Bled like crazy. I felt like Buffy the Vampire Slayer. Why? You thinking of getting one?"

I shuddered. Not in this life.

" 'Cause if you are, Tattoo 4 U 2 is having a special. With every body piercing you get one free tattoo."

Tattoos? Should I ask?

"Want to see mine?"

Was I a masochist? Apparently. "Why not," I said.

Jazz wrenched her right boot off and stuck her foot in my face. Talk about fumes. "Can you tell what it is?" she asked.

Nostrils plugged, I peered closer at her ankle. There it was, a tiny tattoo. "A blood drop?" I ventured. Seemed appropriate.

"No." She shoved it closer to me. "It's a ladybug. See the spots?"

Only before my eyes. I squinted. "Oh, yeah. Cool." Okay, I admit it. It was sort of cool. "Did that hurt?"

"Naw. The other one did. The one on my . . . you know." She wiggled her eyebrows. "I won't show you."

"Thank you."

She laughed. As she tugged her boot back on, her gaze drifted down to her watch again. "Sixteen minutes. This isn't so bad. You want to talk about my hair, too? 'Cause you keep staring at it."

My face seared fireball red. Eyes dropping to my stack of books, I pulled out the peer counselor folder and opened it. My hands shook. What am I doing here? I wondered. I can't do this.

Jazz said, "Maybe we should start with our names. I'm Jasmine Luther. Everybody calls me Jazz, don't ask me why." She drummed the table with her index fingers like a rock musician then shined those sparkling teeth at me again.

It almost made me laugh. Almost. "I'm Antonia Dillon."

Jazz stuck out her hand to shake. "Nice to meet you, Tone."

I flinched.

Jazz leaned back in her chair. "Why don't you tell me about you first. Then maybe I won't be so nervous."

She was nervous? My hands were about to register on the Richter scale. "Okay. My name is Antonia. Everybody calls me Antonia." My eyes met hers.

She shrugged.

I continued, "I'm fourteen and in the eighth grade. My favorite subjects are algebra and history. I'm on the honor roll and in math club . . . I *was* in math club. I had to quit. I used to do gymnastics, too, but—"

Jazz yawned audibly. She checked her watch. "Time sure flies when you're having fun." Batting mascara-caked eyelashes at me, she added, "And that's about all the fun I can stand for one day." She stood.

I stumbled to my feet. As I shoved my notebook back into my bag, she flounced by me and opened the door. "Hey, thanks a lot, Tone," she said at my back. "I feel better already."

Wonderful, I thought. I feel sick.

Chapter 2

I rushed to the school counseling center to catch Dr. DiLeo before he left for the day. Good, he was still in. "It's not going to work, Dr. DiLeo." Standing in the doorway, panting, I added, "She's beyond help."

Dr. DiLeo straddled the desk corner and motioned me to sit. "Now, Antonia," he said. "No one is beyond help." Over the top of his wire-rimmed glasses he studied me. "Hmmm?"

I shifted uncomfortably. "She's not my peer, Dr. DiLeo." I almost blurted, She doesn't have a peer. Instead, what came out of my mouth was "I don't think I'm cut out to be a peer counselor."

"The first session is always tough. Believe me. You probably felt as if nothing was accomplished, right? But you'd be surprised how much progress was made. Just knowing someone cares is self-affirming, Antonia. Truly."

"That's just it," I said. "I don't care." Heat fried my face. There. I'd said it. Now he'd have to remove me from the program. I had no compassion at all.

"Let's just say that with Jazz, there's more than meets the eye."

I widened my eyes at him. "That's a scary thought."

He laughed. Standing up and moving toward the door, he said, "You only have to meet twice a week. Give it another session."

What!

He added, "See if you don't change your mind."

It'd take a left-lobe lobotomy to change my mind.

He smiled. The peppermint bit my nose. I smiled back, even though I wanted to retch.

All the way home I fumed. The only reason I agreed to participate in the peer counseling program was that I could do it during the day. Okay, sure, it was an honor to be asked. And I knew I needed some extracurricular activities on my record if I was going to get into the college-prep program next year. But it was a major sacrifice giving up my homeroom period for peer counseling. Now I'd be up until midnight doing homework. And for who? Or should I say, for what?

Jasmine Luther. She was a what. A subhuman. A foreign body to steer clear of in the hallways. All punkers were. When people found out I was counseling Jasmine Luther, they'd die of hysterics. Of course, you were never supposed to tell who was in counseling; it'd break the oath of confidentiality. But everyone knew. There were no secrets at Oberon Middle School. I'd be the laughingstock. Lead the joke parade. I'd be hung out on the grapevine to wither and die. Nope. No way. Dr. DiLeo couldn't force me.

Could he?

When I flung open the door at home, still muttering to myself, my little brother Chuckie was screaming, "No! I don't want it." Michael, my other brother, hollered at him, "It's all there is, Chuckie. What's the matter? You like Cap'n Crunch."

Chuckie sobbed. "I hate warm milk."

I dropped my backpack on the couch and hustled to the kitchen. "What's going on?" I demanded. "What are you doing home already, Chuckie?"

He pouted.

Michael said, "He was here when I got home. He must've gotten out of day care early."

Without warning, my knees buckled. Exhaustion overwhelmed me as I took in the scene around my brothers. It looked like Hurricane Hugo had swept through the kitchen. Cereal was strewn all over the counter. Dirty dishes filled the sink. Newspapers, envelopes, and trash littered the floor. Automatically, I flicked off the Mr. Coffee. A crust of black had burned to the bottom of the pot. Had Mom left the machine on all day?

"All we got to eat is cereal," Michael said to me. "We're out of milk so I made powdered. Chuckie's being a brat." Michael threatened him with a butter knife.

"Michael!" I stood up, gripped his wrist hard, and yanked away the knife. "Quit it."

Michael took a deep, shaky breath and lowered his arm.

I let go and he crumpled into a chair to eat his cereal. "Chuckie, sweetie, you want to eat it out of the box?" I asked him.

His eyes gleamed. I handed him the box of Cap'n Crunch, which he proceeded to dump all over the floor.

I was too wiped out to care. "Where's Mom?" I asked, wandering over to the refrigerator. "I thought she was going shopping today." The fridge was bare. Except for a bottle of ketchup and a jar of crusty mayonnaise, there was nothing on the shelves. I pulled out the crisper drawer and wished I hadn't. A slimy head of lettuce rolled to the front. "Well?" I turned to Michael.

His face reddened. The freckles on his nose seemed to swell. "She's sick."

"Again?" My anger flared, but I forced it down.

Michael concentrated on his cereal.

"Okay," I said in a sigh. "I'll go get some groceries. Do you want me to call Mrs. Marsh to come over?"

"Yeth," Chuckie said.

"No," Michael countered. "Maybe we could go over there. It's . . . cleaner."

Tears welled in my eyes. It was my fault the house was so bad. I should've cleaned up before leaving this morning. I should've done a load of laundry. I should've checked on Mom. "I'll call Mrs. Marsh," I said, turning away so the boys wouldn't see me cry. They didn't need any more tears.

When I got off the phone, Michael and Chuckie were at it again. Michael was pelting Chuckie with Cap'n Crunch while Chuckie flailed his arms and wailed.

"Stop it, Michael!" I yelled at him.

"Why is it always my fault?" he said.

"You know why." I held his eyes.

He threw the box of cereal across the room and stormed out, screeching, "You're not the boss of me."

"Michael!" My fists clenched. Okay, Antonia, I calmed myself. It's going to be okay. Take a deep breath. They're just kids. In a nicer voice, I called to him, "Michael, take your homework to Mrs. Marsh's, okay?" I knew he wouldn't. He was going to flunk second grade if I didn't keep after him. What did he care?

Chuckie was still howling.

I knelt down in front of him. "Hey, I have something for you."

"A prethent?" He sniffled.

"Yes, a present. Stay put." I bounded to the living room and grabbed my backpack. From inside the front pocket, I fished out the brownie I'd saved from lunch. Not saved, actually. Snitched from an abandoned tray on my way out.

Chuckie tore into the napkin wrapper.

"Save some for Michael," I said.

Michael reappeared in the doorway. Hastily he started picking up pieces of Cap'n Crunch. "He doesn't have to," Michael muttered, but I saw him eyeing the brownie.

"I'll buy brownie mix at the store," I told him.

"And some bread and peanut butter for lunch," Michael said. "We ran out two days ago."

"What've you been eating?"

He shrugged. "I just borrow stuff."

Oh, no. I should've noticed. At least Chuckie's lunch was provided. I removed Mom's Visa card from her billfold and scrounged around in the bottom of her purse for bus fare.

As soon as I dropped off the boys at the neighbor's, I was out of there. If I didn't have to take care of Chuckie and Michael, I'd never come back.

Chapter 3

My eyelids fluttered. Regaining consciousness, I heard someone at the table behind me snoring. Was he mocking me? Had I been snoring? I whipped my chin up off my chest as Mrs. Bartoli finished her introduction to chapter 10, Quadratic Equations.

The bell rang and Mrs. Bartoli said, "Your take-home tests are due today. Leave them on my desk on your way out." The sound of perforated paper being torn from notebooks punctuated the stale air.

It was the last assignment I'd tackled this morning. At one-thirty A.M. By the time I got home from grocery shopping, made the boys dinner, supervised Chuckie in the tub, stood over Michael while he groused about doing homework, got everyone to bed, and cleaned up the house, it was after midnight.

My paper was a mess, all smeared with erasure marks. It embarrassed me to turn it in. I waited until the room cleared before approaching my advanced algebra teacher. "If you can't read this, Mrs. Bartoli, I'll be glad to copy it over," I said.

She glanced down at the paper, then up at me. "You didn't type it?"

My cheeks flared.

"I'm kidding, Antonia. It's fine."

"Are you sure?"

She laughed. "Half the class didn't even do the assignment. And you're worried if I can read your answers?" She chuckled again.

I didn't think it was funny. "Do you want me to type it? I could reserve a PC at lunchtime."

Mrs. Bartoli slapped her hand over mine—the one hastily retrieving the top sheet from a slim stack of test papers. "It was a joke, Antonia. I'm just teasing you." She arched both eyebrows. "Can't you take a joke?"

Sure, when it's funny, I almost said. I hated being teased. At the door I stopped and whirled. "Next time I'll type it."

She met my eyes and frowned.

"Just kidding, Mrs. Bartoli. Can't you take a joke?" I smirked inwardly and left.

At home that night I opened a box of Banquet fried chicken and whipped up some instant mashed potatoes.

Real gourmet. It used to be, when Mom got home from work, she'd cook. Or leave me instructions on the days she had evening appointments.

Was she still sleeping? I wondered at the ceiling. No one could sleep this long and live. It didn't look like she'd even gotten up to make coffee.

Maybe she was dead. That'd be perfect. Leave us without *any* parents. At least there'd be one less mouth to feed. Antonia! I chided myself. You're a terrible person.

"I got a note from my teacher that you gotta sign," Michael said at my side. He shoved a slip of paper under my nose.

It was a permission slip to go to the Museum of Natural History tomorrow. The slip had to be signed by a parent or guardian.

My eyes locked with Michael's. He said, "I left it with Mom, but I guess she forgot. If I don't get it signed, I can't go and I'll have to stay in the liberry all day."

My jaw clenched. "Give me your pencil."

Michael handed me his stub.

As I scribbled my name, as illegibly as possible, I said, "If your teacher asks, tell her I'm your guardian." Which wasn't a total lie.

He wiped his runny nose on his sleeve and took back the slip. Then he shuffled out to the TV.

We ate in the living room while watching *Wheel of Fortune*. By seven o'clock I was getting worried, so I scraped together what was left from dinner and took a plate up to Mom's bedroom. The sun had set and eerie shadows fell across her rumpled bedding.

For a moment I just stood in the doorway and stared. Why, I didn't know. It was a familiar sight. When the lump in bed stirred, I said softly, "Mom? You awake?"

"Who is it?" Mom shot up. "Kurt, is that you?"

"No, Mom. It's me. Antonia." Your slave child, I thought.

Mom fell back on the pillow.

"I brought you some dinner." Forcing a smile, I fibbed, "It's Kentucky Fried. Your favorite."

She rolled back over. "I'm not hungry," she mumbled.

"Okay, fine." I set the plate on her dresser, harder than I meant to. A chicken wing jumped off. It slid across a stack of pictures that had been spread out all over the bureau. Most of the pictures were of Mom and Dad when they were younger. The chicken wing left a greasy smear on one of the pictures.

I started to wipe it off, then noticed it was a picture of us at Christmas. Mom was sitting in front of the tree, hugging Michael. She looked like she was pregnant with Chuckie, so it must've been . . . three years ago? Yeah, must've been. Mom was wearing a Santa hat. I remembered she'd put on the whole Santa suit earlier in the day when Michael declared, "There's no stupid Santa Claus. Tyler told me." I remembered her saying to me, as she buckled the belt, "I want him to believe. Just one more year."

She'd looked pretty convincing with her big belly. Especially going around the house ho-ho-ho-ing in this deep voice. Silly. But Mom was always doing crazy stuff like that. She was so happy that whole time she was pregnant.

In the picture I was sitting beside Mom, holding up a

new sweater set that Santa had brought. I still wore that set occasionally, even though it was way too tight.

Dad must've taken the picture, since he wasn't in it. That was the last Christmas before . . .

My eyes strayed up to Mom's mirror. I freaked. For a second, I thought I saw him. Then I realized it was only me. Mom always said I had Dad's eyes and crooked smile.

The smile faded and all I saw was this tired-looking person with stringy brown hair hanging in her eyes. Mom would be horrified if she saw how long my hair had gotten. Maybe I was hoping she'd notice.

She let out a little whimper and I looked down at her. A wave of sympathy washed over me. "Try to eat, Mom," I said. "You need to keep your strength up."

"Why?" she asked.

When I didn't answer, she exhaled loudly and sat up.

"Did you take your medicine today?" I asked.

She raked her fingers through her hair. In reply, she said, "Hand me my cigarettes, will you, Antonia?"

I glanced down at her nightstand. An ashtray overflowed with cigarette butts. When had she started smoking again? I wondered. Then I saw a big black mark where a lit cigarette had burned a hole. Great. Now I'd have trouble sleeping, worrying whether she was going to set the house on fire.

"You're out of cigarettes," I lied, noticing that the pack had fallen behind the nightstand.

Mom clucked in disgust and stood up. "Run down to the 7-Eleven and get me a couple of packs, okay?"

"They won't sell cigarettes to me. You know that."

She mumbled some obscenity. Then she dragged past me and headed for the bathroom. "You're going to have to be more help around here, Antonia," she snapped on her way past. "I can't do everything myself." She slammed the door in my face.

Chapter 4

Jazz was late for our Friday session. Good, I thought. Maybe she realized how ridiculous this arrangement was, too, and dropped out. It'd be like her. Did Dr. DiLeo actually expect Jazz Luther to honor her agreement to put in fifteen hours? I wondered what she'd done to deserve the punishment.

With a *whoosh,* the door flew open and Jazz swept in. "I'm late. I know," she said, flopping into the chair catty-corner from me. "My watch crapped out. Crap."

She tapped an inch-long, blood-red fingernail on the watch crystal and held her wrist up to her ear.

"Well," I said. "I think our time is up."

She blinked at me and burst into laughter. Jabbing my

shoulder with one of those lethal talons, she replied, "You're bode."

"What?"

"Bode," she repeated. "You know, bode." She clucked her tongue. "It's, like, okay, acceptable, cool." Jazz flipped her frizzy hair over her shoulder.

"Thanks," I muttered. "I'm, like, honored."

She curled a lip.

She looked different today. What was it? Her clothes were the same, maybe a low-cut tank top under the purple jacket. Same shredded jeans and boots. Wait. The hair.

"Like it?" Jazz asked. "That's why I'm late. I ditched lunch and went to my mane man instead." She twisted her head and ran her palm along the hairless left side. Her scalp had been shaved from ear to crown. One side only.

"It's, uh . . ."

"Bode, right?"

Mowed was more like it.

Jazz grinned. "My parents are going to cronk."

Cronk? Geez, we didn't even speak the same language. I knew what she meant, though.

"They'll probably ground me for life," she said. "Which would suit me fine because I'd be outta there. Away from that rat hole."

How far away? I wanted to ask, but didn't. Instead I said, "You really think your parents will ground you?" Maybe she wouldn't make it to school Monday. Or the day after. Or ever again.

Jazz sighed. "I wish." She tipped back in her chair and

plunked her feet on the table. "They'll just yell and threaten to send me to prep school. Again. Or to my sister Janey's. Then I'll tell them how, when they dumped me on her last summer, she totally corrupted me by taking me out partying. And if they weren't neglecting me so bad I'd be normal. You know, lay the old guilt trip on 'em."

"Do you really talk to your parents that way?" I asked.

"Course. Don't you?"

"No way."

"What, they'd smack you?"

My face flared. "No, my parents never hit me. They've never laid a hand on me."

Jazz removed her feet and leaned forward. "Never? Not even to, like, hug you?"

Our eyes met briefly before mine dropped. This is a total waste of time, I thought. Exhaling exasperation or weariness or both, I riffled through my backpack for my counseling folder.

Jazz said, "I'm sorry. Sometimes my mouth takes off without my brain. So, your parents don't hit you. That's good. At least *that's* not your problem."

"Look." I slapped the folder on the table. "We're not here to talk about *my* problems. We're here to help *you.*"

Jazz smiled. "So, you admit you *have* problems."

I wrenched the folder off the table and stood. "I'm leaving. If you're not going to take this seriously, then let's just forget it. I have better things to do."

"Like what?" She sneered. "Homework?"

"Yes, like homework. I'm giving up my homeroom for

you, which means I have to do homework at night, which means I don't get to bed until late, which means—"

She cut me off. "Let me guess. You got a permanent case of PMS?"

She must've felt the fire shooting from my eyes because she said, "Hey, chill, Tone. Just because I'm joking around doesn't mean I'm not serious. Haven't you ever heard of laughing through the tears?" Her voice wavered a little, as if she were on the verge of tears.

It drew me back down to my chair.

Jazz covered her face with her hands and burst out sobbing. Then she hiccuped twice and removed her hands.

She wasn't crying. She was laughing!

She sucked in a fake sob and laughed again.

I lurched to my feet and charged out the door.

"Tone," she yelled after me. "Wait, I'm kidding. Come back."

"Never," I muttered. "I'm never coming back."

"Dr. DiLeo, I can't do this," I told him. "I can't counsel a crazy person. You've got to find someone else."

He leaned forward in his chair, elbows on knees. "What's the problem exactly?"

Exactly? She's on drugs. I couldn't say that, although it was probably the truth. "She mocks me," I said. "She's mocking the whole program. She doesn't take it seriously."

He shook his head sadly. "I thought if anyone could reach her, you could."

That made me feel bad. Like she was doomed without me.

He met my eyes. "Did you start at step one on the list? Trying to find something you have in common?"

"We never got to step one," I replied. "She's so . . ." I couldn't even come up with a word.

Dr. DiLeo offered, "Unique?"

That wasn't it. Weird. Whacked. Freaky. Punk. "We don't have anything in common," I said. Thank God, I didn't add.

Dr. DiLeo straightened his wire-rims. "I bet you could find something," he said. "You've met twice. What have you talked about?"

"Nothing," I answered. "I mean, she does all the talking. She told me how I could get a free tattoo with a body piercing."

He rolled his eyes. "Do you want me to sit in on the session?"

"No!" That'd be worse, I thought. She'd never show me her tattoos. "I want you to find someone else. I'm not the right person for—"

"You're the perfect person, Antonia," he said, cutting me off. "You're responsible, intelligent, caring . . ."

"You can't find anyone else, can you?"

"How'd you guess?" He grinned.

I glared.

Dr. DiLeo sobered and said, "Maybe if you opened up a little, she would, too. I know she comes on strong, but you have to take control, Antonia. Start slow. Talk about school or your family. That should be something you can both get into. I bet if you share your feelings, she'll share hers."

Share my feelings? No way. Not with her.

Dr. DiLeo reached out and touched my arm. I recoiled. "You can do this, Antonia. I know you can. She needs your help. *I* need your help."

Yeah, everyone in the world needed my help. So who was helping me?

Chapter 5

My bus broke down on the way home, so I was half an hour late. The house was quiet when I rushed in. Too quiet. And it smelled like smoke. "Michael? Chuckie?" I dropped my pack in the hall and raced to the kitchen.

Mom was there, sitting at the kitchen table with Chuckie in her lap. It looked as if she'd just trimmed his hair. Good, he needed it worse than me. "Hello, Antonia." She smiled up at me.

"Mom."

"I'm sorry for what I said last night," she began. "I know you're doing the best you can. We all are." She smiled weakly, like it hurt.

I wanted to rush over and hug her. But I couldn't. My feet wouldn't move.

Mom started rocking Chuckie and humming. That's when I noticed what he was doing.

"Chuckie!" I charged across the room and grabbed the scissors out of his hands. Naturally he screamed bloody murder. "You'll cut yourself," I told him. "Here." I retrieved a dump truck from under the table. "Play with this."

Chuckie squirmed out of Mom's lap and zoomed his truck over my foot and across the floor. Mom lit up a cigarette.

"What's that smell?" I asked.

"Oh, we had a slight accident." She waved toward the stove. The stove top was empty, but a smoking pan lay in the sink. Something was burned to the bottom. "I was going to make us all eggs and bacon," she added. "Guess I forgot how to cook." She sort of chuckled.

Wow. It'd been a while since she'd actually cooked us dinner. I noticed she was wearing a dress and had combed her hair. Maybe she was better. My spirits lifted.

The ashes from her cigarette floated to the floor and settled on a pile of laundry. "Where's Michael?" I asked, shoveling up the laundry to save us from a flash fire.

"I sent him to McDonald's."

"Alone?"

She blinked down at me. Her eyes filled with tears. "I'm a terrible mother." She covered her face and burst into tears.

I'm sorry, I'm sorry, I apologized silently. "No, you're not. He'll be okay. I'm just a big worrywart. You know me." It was meant to reassure her, although I didn't feel reassured.

Mom continued to cry while I separated the whites from the colors. Then I remembered we were out of detergent. For some reason it made me mad at Mom. Stop it, I scolded myself. She's sick. She can't help it.

Feeling guilty, I rose and walked back to the fridge. "Do you want eggs and bacon? I can make you some."

Mom snuffled. "No, thank you."

"Mom," I said. "You have to eat."

She lowered her hands and held my eyes for as long as she could, which was about a second.

"You have to," I repeated.

Taking a deep breath, she stubbed out her cigarette and said, "Eggs and bacon would taste good."

"Good." I smiled at her. Better. She is better. Inside the fridge, an opened package of bacon lay on the top shelf, half frozen and uncovered. It must've been in the freezer for a year. Did bacon go bad? What if I poisoned her? Yeah, what if? Antonia! Quit it.

Just then Michael returned with two bags of food. Thank you, God, I prayed. "Why don't we have eggs and bacon some other time?" I said to Mom, shutting the door. "We don't want to waste a real meal deal."

Mom laughed. "What would I do without you, Antonia?"

Good question, I thought. I took a bag from Michael and began unloading.

Mom ate one french fry and shoved the rest away. Rising wearily, she said, "I think I'll go lie down for a while. I'm not really hungry." At the door she turned and said, "Oh,

Antonia. I had to use some of your savings to pay the electric bill."

A box of supersize fries slipped from my hand and scattered all over the floor.

Don't think about the money. Don't! I ordered myself. Think about something else.

I switched off my light and climbed into bed. Jazz materialized in my mind. Good. I wasn't happy about counseling her, but I couldn't let Dr. DiLeo down. Not if he really needed my help. And I was curious about Jazz's real problem, don't ask me why. The vision of her bald scalp came into view. I could just imagine her parents cronking. For some reason it made me smile, and I drifted off to sleep.

Over the weekend, I studied my peer counseling notes and handouts, and even practiced a few approaches. Dr. DiLeo was right: I needed to take control. That was the main thing, getting past step one.

When I yanked open the conference room door, Jazz was already there. She had earplugs on and was rocking out to music from her hand-held CD player. Probably some obscene shock rock. Her eyes were closed and her fingers tapped across the table as if she were working the keyboard. She didn't even notice I'd come in.

I lifted an earplug and said, "Hello? Anybody home?"

She jerked back to reality and flicked off her CD player. Quickly, she dropped it into her jacket pocket. Too quickly. Which made me wonder where she'd stolen it.

I said, "Okay, Jazz. Let's get going."

"You go ahead." She slumped across the table. "Wake me up in an hour." She covered her head with her hands.

Take control, I ordered myself. "I want you to answer some questions."

She grunted.

I began at the top of my list. "What's your favorite color?"

She twisted her head toward me. "Black," she said.

I jotted down her answer.

"What's yours?" she asked.

My pen paused midair. "I don't know. White, I guess."

She lifted her head and snorted. "White is the absence of color. Duh."

Control, I reminded myself. "What's your favorite subject in school?"

"Lunch," she said.

I snorted. "Seriously."

"Seriously?" She cocked her head. "Lunch."

I exhaled wearily. The urge to get up and go was strong, but I forced myself to forge ahead. "Do you have any brothers or sisters? Besides Janey."

She blinked. "How'd you know about Janey?"

"You said you stayed with her last summer. She took you to a party."

Jazz rolled her eyes. "I lied. Janey wouldn't know a party if it crashed at her house and burned her butt. She doesn't know what fun is. She's just soooo special. So perfect. She reminds me of you."

Just as I was about to spear her with my pen, she added, "But I still love her. You know?"

That brought me up short. Blinking away from Jazz's piercing gaze, I wrote down, *Janey. Perfect.*

"In answer to your question," Jazz said, "I have only the one perfect sister. How about you?"

"No sisters," I said. "Two little brothers."

"Lucky." She sounded as if she meant it.

"Oh, yeah," I replied sarcastically.

"What? You don't like them? Are they brats or something?"

I shrugged. "Sometimes."

"Like how?"

I sighed. "Do you mind? I'm asking the questions."

Jazz threw up her hands. "Sorr-ee. What is this, let's play police interrogation?"

I just looked at her. She probably was an expert on police interrogation.

She held up her right palm. "Continue, Officer Dillon. I promise to tell the truth."

A snicker might have escaped my lips. "Who's your favorite teacher?"

She choked. "You're kidding, right?"

I waited.

"Well, wow. I just can't pick a favorite. There are so many to love." She studied her blood-red nails. "All teachers hate me. Surprise!" She framed her face with spread-out fingers.

Checking that question off my list, I muttered, "I can't imagine why."

"What?" Jazz glared at me.

I didn't answer.

"You mean the way I dress?" she said. "How I look? So what? It's a free country. My body is my temple. I can decorate it any way I want."

"Don't expect anyone to worship at your altar," I mumbled.

She tossed her one side of hair over her shoulder and added, "My clothes are who I am. They make a statement."

Yeah: Stay back, I might be contagious. I didn't say it. What I did say was "What you see is what you get."

Jazz shot to her feet. "What's that supposed to mean?"

I was afraid she was going to attack me. Really. No telling what weapons she had stashed in that leather jacket. Switchblades, handguns. Before I could escape, Jazz shoved her chair away and clomped over to the heater. Folding her arms and staring out the window, she said, "I'm not an imbecile, you know. People shouldn't judge other people by the way they look."

"Probably not," I said. "But they do. Surprise!" I framed my face.

She twisted around and glared at me, then twisted back.

I checked my watch. Another twenty minutes to go? We were getting nowhere. "Okay, so you don't have a favorite teacher." What was the next question on my list?

"Do you?" she said.

My mind shifted back. "Mrs. Bartoli, I guess."

"That witch?" Jazz said.

I shot eye-bullets at Jazz. "She's a great teacher."

"Oh, yeah." Jazz clomped back to her chair. "First day of class I walk in and she sends me straight to the office."

"Why? What did you do?"

Jazz batted her eyelashes at me. "What'd I do? I was born."

Okay, it was a stupid question. Mrs. Bartoli didn't put up with any crap. It was one of the reasons I liked her. Class was calm. We could learn without having to dodge spit wads or feel faint from nail polish fumes. Jazz must've said or done something, though.

"I didn't say or do anything," she said, as if reading my mind. " She just hated me from day one. I got A's on all my tests and she still gave me a C for my final grade. She said I had an attitude problem." Jazz stuck out her tongue. Was that a stud glistening on the tip?

It took me a second to stop shuddering. Wow, I thought. That didn't seem fair. If Jazz had earned an A, she should've gotten one.

"Teachers." Jazz rolled her eyes. "They're all alike. Every adult is. They always judge you on the way you look, not who you are."

"I thought you said the way you look *is* who you are."

She met my eyes and frowned. "That's not what I meant."

My eyes dropped to my list. Next question?

"I bet you get straight A's," Jazz said.

I didn't answer.

"Yeah, I figured. Just like Janey. Suck-ups rule."

That was it. I slapped my folder closed, got up, and stormed to the door. Wrenching it open, I snarled, "I earn my A's."

"Yeah? Well, so do I," she snarled back.

Chapter 6

A pink slip came for me during history class. The message summoned me to Dr. DiLeo's office immediately. Good. It'd save me from having to stop by after school. I hated giving up so easily, but Jazz and I were never going to make it past step one. She was so crazy, she was making me crazy. Pretty soon that'd be the one thing we had in common.

Dr. DiLeo's door was ajar, so I knocked lightly. His voice carried through the crack. "Come."

When I pushed in the door, my chin hit the floor. Jazz twirled around in Dr. DiLeo's chair. "Hey, Tone," she said with a wave.

I bristled.

"Antonia, come in," Dr. DiLeo said from the student seat. "We were just talking about you."

My whole body tensed.

"Shut the door," he added.

I eased the door closed behind me. Turning back around, I began, "Dr. DiLeo—"

He held up a hand. His eyes widened on Jazz.

She smiled somberly. "I'm sorry about today. I was an ass. An assho—"

"We get the picture," Dr. DiLeo said.

My eyes focused on him. He looked at me, sort of helplessly. "Okay." He stood. "I'll leave you two to work this out."

"No!" I moved to block his exit. "I can't do this, Dr. DiLeo." My voice lowered to a murmur. "She's a psycho."

Jazz howled, "See, DiLeo? I told you she was good. She already has me figured out."

He pointed a stiff finger at Jazz. "That's *Dr. DiLeo* to you. Show some respect."

Jazz curled a lip at me. She stood and saluted him. "Yes, suh!"

Dr. DiLeo searched my face. He must've picked up on my panic, or sense of helplessness, because he resumed his seat and said, "Let's set some ground rules. First of all, you both need to respect each other's space. You're very different people—"

"No duh," Jazz interrupted.

He shot her a warning look. "But that doesn't mean one of you is better than the other. Or right. Or wrong."

Jazz's eyes hit the floor the same time mine did.

"Second," he said, "you understand the oath of confidentiality. There's a reason for it. It allows you to speak freely. So speak freely. Be honest. Trust that whatever you say goes no further than your peer counselor's ears."

Jazz snorted.

"Third," he said, ignoring her, "listen. Discuss. Don't react. If you disagree with something the other person says or believes, that's fine. Everyone's entitled to his or her opinion. There's no need to go running out of the room." He locked in on me.

My eyes burned holes in the knees of his khakis.

He paused a minute, then added, "I have an assignment for both of you. I want you to answer this question: If you could change one thing about your life, what would it be?"

Jazz's eyes met mine and we both blinked away.

Dr. DiLeo stood up. "I'll leave you to think about that." Somehow he slipped out around me.

Jazz made a face at his back. "Stupid," she said. "Does he think we're in kindergarten?"

"Apparently," I mumbled.

She shook her head. "Such a wasted question. If I could change the shit in my life, I would. What's the use of talking about stuff you can't change?" She looked at me. "So, what would you change?"

"Everything," I said.

Her eyebrows arched.

"But you're right," I added quickly. "What's the use of talking about things you can't change?"

Jazz hoisted herself up onto Dr. DiLeo's desk and spun in a circle on her rear. "You want to look through his confidential files? See who's whacking out? I could probably pick the lock."

My eyes narrowed.

"Just kidding. God, Antonia, you take everything so seriously. Wait." She held up a hand. "Don't get mad. Look, from now on if I'm joking, I'll hold up two fingers." She demonstrated with the first two fingers of her right hand. "Like, peace, man."

"And what if you have to go poopie?" Why'd I say that? Probably because two fingers is Chuckie's signal.

Jazz exploded in laughter. She hiccuped so hard she bounced right off Dr. DiLeo's desk. "You are so bode, Tone. There's hope for you yet." She held up two fingers.

What'd that mean? Before I could ask, the bell rang. As I opened the door to leave, Jazz breezed by and socked me on the shoulder. "See ya Friday," she said.

I missed three problems on my algebra test. *Three problems.* Mrs. Bartoli arched an eyebrow when she handed it back Friday morning. A big fat C pulsated from the top of the page. I'd never gotten a C in my life. Jazz maybe, but not me. For a long time, I just sat there and stared at the grade. While Mrs. Bartoli worked the problems on the board, my mind went numb. My whole body went numb. A C? A C meant average. A C meant failure.

After class, Mrs. Bartoli stopped me at the door. "Antonia, is something wrong?" she asked.

"I got a C," I replied.

"I know," she said. "And you never handed in the problems from page one sixty-five."

My eyes widened. "I didn't?"

Mrs. Bartoli furrowed her brow. "I'm worried about you, Antonia. This isn't like you."

No kidding. I'd had Mrs. Bartoli last year for beginning algebra, so she knew I was a straight-A student.

"I'm just tired," I said. "I have a lot of stuff on my mind."

"I've noticed that. Maybe you should talk to a counselor. I hear Dr. DiLeo—"

"It won't happen again," I said, cutting her off. I had to get out of there fast. "I'll do an extra page of problems tonight. Bye," I said and ran.

Jazz sat on top of the conference table, legs crossed Indian style. Her eyes were closed and her hands rested on her thighs, palms up. "Ohmmm," she said, or something like that.

"If you're sick, we can skip today's session." My heart raced hopefully.

"Ohmmm," she droned again. Without opening her eyes, Jazz said, "Join me."

Was she nuts?

She twisted her head and cracked an eyelid. "Come on. Why not?"

Why not? Because after the age of two, there is an unwritten rule that says you are not to sit on tables. You are not to sit on tables and hum. We'd get busted if anyone walked in. Besides, it looked stupid.

"Ohmmm," she intoned.

So far the day was a total loss. I felt tense as a tightrope, and I wasn't getting anywhere with my list of questions. So why not? Setting my backpack on the chair, I used the seat as a step up.

My legs didn't cooperate when I commanded them to form a pretzel like Jazz's. They were too long and stiff. It was unnatural. Jazz reached over and tucked my ankles over my thighs. "It's called the lotus position," she said.

"Maybe on you. Ow." I stretched my skirt down over my knees.

"Ohmmm," Jazz intoned again.

Was I supposed to *ohmmm?*

Jazz whispered, "Close your eyes. Relax completely. Hold your palms up, thumb and index finger touching, and start your mantra."

My mantra?

"Ohmmm," she droned.

"Ohmmm," I droned. Then again. "Ohmmm." I couldn't help it. I started to giggle.

Jazz twisted her head and smirked. "My mother read that parents should spend quality time with their children. One way is to sign up for organized activities together. This month we're taking meditation to free the mind. Last month it was Rolfing. Have you ever Rolfed, Tone?"

"Only after the school's shepherd's pie," I said.

She laughed. She laughed so hard she lost her lotus. When she finally sobered, she said, "My father's in on the torture, too. He took me to the driving range. Talk about mindfree."

I smiled. To me it sounded like heaven. "Belly dancing."

"What?" Jazz turned to me.

Did I say that out loud? "I, uh, remember once my mom and I took this belly-dancing class at the rec center. She made me practice with her at home in the living room. It was hilarious. I was terrible, but she was pretty good."

"Your mom sounds cool. Think she'd teach me to belly dance?"

My throat caught. "That was a long time ago. She probably doesn't remember. What's the problem with spending time with your parents?" I asked.

She just looked at me. Then she sighed and said, "The problem is they don't pick anything I want to do."

Ah. Like drug dealing? Body piercing? "Maybe you could get matching tattoos," I suggested.

Jazz jabbed me. "I'll tell them my peer counselor advised it."

"Oh, please."

"So." She swiveled on her rear to face me. "Who do you hang with?" She hugged her knees.

Hang with? I hadn't been convicted of a major crime yet, so no cell mates. "What do you mean?"

"You know, friends. Girlfriends, boyfriends."

Hey, that was one of the questions on my list. Maybe this was working. "Can we get off the table now?" I asked—pleaded with my eyes.

Jazz flung herself to the floor. I slid down after her. Once we were settled in our seats, Jazz removed her boots and flopped her bare feet up on the table. "Well?" she said, leaning back. "Are you going to answer my question?"

Scraping my stare away from her striped toenails, I thought, Why do I always end up answering my own questions? Rummaging in my backpack for my folder, I replied, "You wouldn't know my friends."

"Try me."

I met her eyes. "Okay. Lindy Meeks."

"Yeah, I know Lindz. I thought she moved."

Did she? I hadn't talked to her since before Christmas break. Come to think of it, I hadn't seen her around for the last couple of months.

"Tamra Dundee-Kelso," I said.

Jazz frowned. "I don't know her."

"See?" How could she? Tamra was my friend in elementary school. She didn't even go to Oberon.

"Is that it?" Jazz asked.

"No."

But it was. I mean, there were a few people I talked to in class, if necessary. There was math club. But only four people had joined, and even though we met twice a week, we mostly played math games. You can't have personal discussions when your mind is on math. Anyway, I'd quit math club in November.

Every once in a while Mrs. Bartoli ate lunch with me. I couldn't name her. "Who do you hang with?" I said instead.

Jazz counted on her fingers. "D.J. Eakers, a.k.a. the Eeks; Animal Montrose; Martina Romero; Cam 'the Ram' Ramsey. Marisa Fabrero, except she has a death wish, so I try to stay out of her way." Jazz paused to take a breath.

"What do you mean, she has a death wish?"

Jazz's nose wrinkled. "She smokes. Not just cigarettes either, which are poison enough."

That surprised me. "Don't you smoke?"

"You think I'm crazy? Oh, yeah, you do. Psycho, wasn't it?"

My face burned.

She went on, "My grandma Ruth died of lung cancer. If you ever saw anyone die that way, you'd never light up. Do you smoke?"

"Of course not."

"Good. Because if you did, I just couldn't respect you, Tone."

I met her eyes. No mocking gleam; she was serious. "What do you and your friends do? When you hang?"

Jazz shrugged. "You know, we steal and lie, set fire to small children." She blinked at me. Almost in disgust, she held up two fingers. "We just hang. You know, hang."

"Where?" I asked.

"Here, there. Ram's old man built a wood shed in their yard before he split. We fixed it up."

"You mean like Gang Central?"

Jazz laughed. "Right. Gang Central. Anyway, we meet there. Figure stuff out."

"Like what?" I was on a roll now. Pretty soon she'd confess to some major felony. Then her problem would be revealed.

"Like how to present ourselves next week. What to wear, how to do our hair, makeup. We experiment with different looks. Or we talk about deep stuff, like how come Ram's mom started drinking again. And what he's going to do so he doesn't have to quit school and support her, since she just stays home and boozes all day. Or what authority figures we can torment this week. Last week we hung around the bank building by the mall. Talk about shanking out the suits. The security guards made us move, so we camped out at Walgreen's. No one cronked, which was a drag. Then we tried to use the earphones at CDeez Happen until the manager told us to split."

Was that it? No drug deals? No gang bangs?

Jazz snapped her fingers. "Oh, yeah. And afterward we went to the park and set fire to small children." Jazz looked at me. She held up two fingers.

"I know you're kidding," I said. At least, I hoped she was.

Chapter 7

For dinner Sunday night I made eggs and bacon. Couldn't let the bacon go to waste. It was the worst idea I ever had. The sizzle and smell of bacon brought back memories. Memories of Sundays when we were all together. The old days. The good days. Tears blurred my vision, and I blinked them back. So what? Forget it, I battled my brain. Those days were long gone. We'd never have another family Sunday.

My eyes strayed to the calendar on the refrigerator as my vision cleared. Today's date was blacked out with magic marker. March 19. Mom and Dad's wedding anniversary.

A shiver raced up my spine. I turned off the stove, charged upstairs, and flung open Mom's door. She was a lump again, but I could see the sheets rise and fall. My heart restarted.

I wanted to rush over and crawl into bed with her, the way I used to when I was little. When nightmares would wake me up in the middle of the night and I'd run to my parents' room.

You're not little now, a voice in my head said. Besides, there's only her and it wouldn't be the same. The nightmares didn't scare me anymore. Not as much as waking up.

While the boys watched TV, I took a shower then lay on my bed, memorizing my book talk for lit class tomorrow. The book was *The True Confessions of Charlotte Doyle,* which I had liked better the first time I read it, in sixth grade. The only part I could really get into was the ending where Charlotte runs away from her family.

My mind wandered and pretty soon I was thinking about Jazz. I couldn't figure her out. Yeah, sure, she was a psycho. She admitted that. But she didn't seem all that troubled. Maybe the trouble was me. I was a poor peer counselor.

No, I didn't want to believe that. That would mean failure. I couldn't fail. I wouldn't. And I couldn't let Dr. DiLeo down.

But Jazz was so manipulative. She was probably using me. Showing up to put in her time. For some reason, I didn't think that was true. But it wouldn't be the first time I'd been made fun of. Tamra told me once we were called the ya-ya girls by everyone in school. I didn't know what she meant. What's a ya-ya? All I knew was I had responsibilities. People counted on me. People expected me to do the right thing. I had goals and ideals, too. Straight A's were more than an achievement; they were a necessity. They were my escape, the only way I could graduate early and go to college. If all my college money wasn't used up paying bills.

My temper flared. How could Mom use *my* money? It was so unfair. I didn't want to think about it. I didn't want to think about Jazz either.

Tamra. My friend.

Springing to my feet, I raced down the stairs to the telephone in the kitchen. It was still early, quarter to eight. Tamra'd probably be doing homework. It'd been a while since I'd talked to her, so I had to look up her number. After two rings, someone picked up. "Hello?"

The voice sounded familiar. "Hello, is this Shelley?"

There was silence on the other end.

"Hello?" I said again.

"Who's this?"

Maybe it wasn't Tamra's older sister. Maybe it was . . . "Tamra?"

"Yeah."

"Hi, it's Antonia. You sound more like Shelley every day."

Silence again. Tamra said, "I guess you haven't heard. Shelley's . . . dead."

"What?" My heart stopped. "When? What happened? How did she die?"

"I really don't want to talk about it," Tamra said quietly. "Anyway, it's old news."

"When did it happen?" I asked.

"Like the beginning of last summer."

"Last summer? Why didn't you call me?"

"I did." Her voice rose in response to mine. "You were at the library or something. I left a message with your mom."

My mom? She never told me. "I never got it, Tamra. I swear."

"I wondered why you didn't call me back."

I didn't know what to say. Shelley dead? Almost a year ago? Where was I? Had I been out of touch that long? My whole body sagged, inside and out. I should've been there for Tamra. She had always been there for me when I needed her. Especially three years ago, when everything happened with Dad. I finally said, "Are you okay?" Dumb, Antonia. Of course she's not okay.

"Yeah, sure," she said. "It was ages ago. Not that it isn't still hard sometimes . . ." She exhaled. "You know. So, how are you?"

"Good," I said. "Except—"

She waited. "What?"

I couldn't burden her with my problems. They were insignificant compared to what she must've gone through. She idolized Shelley. So did I. Shelley was cool. "Nothing," I finally mumbled.

"How's school?" Tamra asked. "Still getting straight A's? Still a ya-ya?"

"Yeah." I let out a short laugh. "How 'bout you?"

"Noooo. I actually got a B in biology last term. Mr. Meklevick, the toad. It's harder here at St. Anne's. I wish I were going to Oberon. Or you could've gone to St. Anne's."

"Me too." The conversation stalled.

"Well, I better go," Tamra said. "My friends are here to practice pom-pom routines. We're trying out for the spirit squad next month. Hey, you still in gymnastics? You'd make it for sure."

"No," I said. "I had to quit."

There was a flurry of activity in the background, someone giggling, calling for Tamra. "I'm coming," Tamra hollered. To me she said, "It was good talking to you, Antonia. Did you call for a reason?"

"Uh, no," I replied. "Just to talk."

"Oh," she said.

After a long moment, I said, "Well, good luck. In the tryouts."

"Thanks. Hey, I'll call you sometime. Okay?"

"Sure, okay," I said to the buzzing phone in my hand.

"Antonia?" Chuckie stood in front of me, tugging on my bathrobe. "Antonia," he whined. "I don't feel so goo—" He didn't even get out the last word before he threw up all over my bare feet.

"What are you doing?" Michael grabbed the pay phone out of my hand.

"I'm calling Mrs. Marsh," I told him. "They won't let us leave the hospital without someone signing a release form."

"You sign it," he said.

I just looked at him. "I can't. It has to be an adult. What's wrong with calling Mrs. Marsh?"

Michael shoved his hands into his pockets. "She's been asking questions again. About Mom."

I hung up the phone.

Now what was I going to do? When Chuckie's temperature reached a hundred and five, the only thing I could think of was to take him to the emergency room. I couldn't even wake up Mom. She must've taken sleeping pills or something.

The doctor said Chuckie was going to be okay, that he just had a flu bug that was going around, but now we were stuck here.

"Michael, go get us a soda," I said, digging out two quarters from my billfold. "I'll think of something."

On my way back to Chuckie's bedside, I ran into the nurse coming out of his room. Before she could ask, I said, "My mom's on her way. She was real worried when she got home from work and we weren't there. She should be here any minute."

The nurse nodded. "He's asleep now," she whispered, glancing over her shoulder at Chuckie. "The doctor gave him something for the fever and vomiting. He should be fine."

Michael appeared at my side with a can of Dr Pepper. He took a swig.

The nurse added, "Why don't you two wait out in the lounge? You'll be more comfortable."

"I'd better stay here," I said.

"Me too," Michael said.

She frowned at Michael. "I'm afraid we have rules—"

Just then a gurney wheeled by. Someone shouted, "Motor vehicle accident. There's two more in transport. Call a trauma code, stat."

The nurse raced down the hall. Instinctively I pulled Michael close.

"Quit it." Michael pushed me away. "You're squishing me."

There was lots of commotion at the end of the hall. Everyone was busy. Perfect, I thought, running into Chuckie's room.

Throwing off his blanket, I lifted Chuckie up and said, "Come on, Michael. We're going home."

Chapter 8

"You look dead," Jazz said as she climbed up onto the conference table and assumed the lotus position. Today she'd smeared black goo under her eyes and wore all black clothing, which matched her lipstick and nails. Talk about looking dead.

"It's been a rough week," I said.

"Tell me about it," Jazz replied.

When neither of us spoke, I looked up at her. "I mean it," she said. "Why don't you tell me about it?"

I shook my head. The silence grew. Jazz stared down at me. It was making me uncomfortable. Just to fill the void, I said, "Okay, since you asked. I spent almost all night Sunday in the emergency room. Then I had to stay home Monday and Tuesday with Chuckie, so I missed handing in another algebra assignment and a history review. I found out my friend Tamra's sister died—"

"Whoa, whoa, whoa." Jazz waved her arms. Her eyes bugged out. "Let's start over. Why were you in the emergency room?"

A weary sigh escaped my lips. "My little brother Chuckie got sick. He had a temperature of a hundred and five and he was throwing up all over the place."

"Eeooh." Jazz stuck out her tongue stud. "Is he all right?"

"Yeah. It's just the flu. He doesn't feel all that great yet, but I sent him to day care today. I couldn't miss any more school. Now Michael will probably get sick. And me." I laid my head on my backpack. A headache threatened to implode my brain.

Jazz slid off the table and walked around behind me. Her fingers dug into my shoulders. "Ouch!" I flinched.

"Relax," she said. "You're so tense. I'll give you a massage. The Jazz Luther special, only thirty-nine dollars and ninety-five cents."

"No, that's okay." I elbowed her away.

"Just put your head down. It's free."

I didn't have the strength to argue. At first it hurt, her fingers piercing my shoulders like stilettos, then the pain eased to a dull ache, until at last her hands felt wonderful. My head stopped threatening eruption. "Where'd you learn to do that?" I asked.

"I told you. Rolfing." She added in a mutter, "I never thought I'd actually use it."

"Maybe you could teach me," I murmured.

"Sure," she said. "Anytime. You know, you do feel like you have a temperature. If you're going to barf, hold up three fingers, okay? This outfit cost a fortune at Goodwill."

I smiled under my arms. "I'll let you know."

"Tell me about Tamra's sister," she added.

I tensed again. Her fingers dug in.

After a long, deep breath I said, "She died last summer. Tamra called to tell me and Mom didn't give me the message." She probably wasn't lucid enough to write it down, I didn't say.

"Typical," Jazz muttered. "How'd she die?"

"I don't know. Tamra wouldn't tell me."

Jazz said, "Probably committed suicide."

My head shot up. "No way." I twisted around.

She shrugged. "You never know."

"I do know." I twisted back. "Shelley wouldn't do that. She wasn't sick or depressed or anything. She was perfectly normal."

"What do you mean?"

I turned around again. "What do you mean, what do I mean?"

"I mean, what's your definition of 'normal'?" she said.

I clucked my tongue. "You know, normal. Happy, healthy. Someone with friends and family. Shelley had all kinds of friends. She was really popular."

"So if you're not popular, you're not normal?"

"I didn't say that." Did I?

Jazz added, "I have friends and family. So I guess I'm normal."

I sighed. "There's more," I said. "You have goals and

dreams. Things you want to do with your life. You value life. You don't waste it." I met Jazz's eyes. "You don't waste yourself."

She shrugged. "I'd agree with that. I'm just saying you never know people. Not really." Her fingers dug in again.

I wriggled out of her grasp and she resumed her seat. Her eyes held mine for a long moment before staring off over my shoulder. "I had a friend in sixth grade who shot himself in the head," she said. "Everyone thought it was an accident, except me. I know he did it on purpose. I could've stopped him, too. I sort of sensed things weren't right. If only I'd called him when he quit hanging out with us. If only I'd been a better friend."

"It's not your fault," I said. "You didn't shoot him."

She met my eyes. "I might as well have." Her head dropped. "We're all responsible. We might as well have put the gun in his hand and pulled the trigger."

"No." I shook my head. "You can't feel responsible for everyone in the world. You can't."

Her head raised and her eyes widened. "Really?"

I widened my eyes back. "Really." Then, more softly, I repeated it. "Really."

"Why did you have to quit math club?" Jazz asked.

"What?" Where'd that come from?

"You said you had to quit math club. How come?"

I didn't remember telling her anything about math club. "It meets after school. I can't stay."

"Why not?"

How did we get on this? It wasn't a subject I cared to discuss. Maybe if I didn't answer, she'd take the hint.

"Well?" she said.

Or not. With an exasperated sigh, I said, "I have to babysit my brothers, okay?"

"Why you? I thought you said Chuckie was in day care."

"He is. But they drop him off at four o'clock."

"Where's your mom?" Jazz reached down and pulled a compact out of the back pocket of her pants, which wasn't easy since they were skintight. "Forget that. Stupid question." She flipped the top open and examined her face in the mirror. "Working, right?" she said.

I shrugged.

"Like most normal parents," she muttered. Clipping the compact closed, she added, "I wish I had brothers."

"You are psycho," I said.

She made a face, her interpretation of a psycho, which was pretty close. I had to smile. "Be careful what you wish for. You might get it."

Jazz said, "I mean it. My parents might not get on my case so bad if there was someone else they could rag on."

"Maybe if you weren't so punk, they wouldn't get on your case."

Jazz narrowed her eyes at me. "If I weren't so 'punk,' as you put it, I wouldn't be me."

I shrugged, but felt rebuffed. Hadn't we been over this?

Jazz retrieved a tube of lipstick from the other pocket. Carefully, meticulously, she spread the black cream on her lips. In the mirror, she pressed her lips together. Then she spread some lipstick under her eyes. With her index finger, she rubbed it in.

"Does that stuff come off?" I asked.

"I hope not." She grinned. "You want some?" She held it out to me.

I recoiled. "No, thanks."

"Come on, try it. It comes off. I promise." She waggled the tube at me.

I licked my lips. I looked at her. It was so ugly, so awful, so tempting. I took the tube.

Jazz held up the mirror. "Wait," she said. She yanked out a Kleenex and wiped off the tip of the lipstick. "I don't want you to get AIDS."

At my expression of horror, she laughed and held up two fingers.

I sneered back. Exhaling a deep breath, I touched the lipstick to my lips. It felt slimy and warm. I'd never put on lipstick before.

"Press a little harder," Jazz said. Her own lips contorted while I spread it on thick.

I studied myself in the mirror. A slow smile crept across my face.

"Bode," Jazz said. "Bode and bad."

"Okay," I told her. "Give me the Kleenex."

"Didn't I mention?" she said. "You need turpentine to take it off."

She didn't hold up two fingers. I could've killed her. She whooped with laughter.

All afternoon I had to hide my gray lips behind my hand. At least at home no one noticed. My lips matched the color of everyone else's, since they'd all come down with the flu.

Chapter 9

We had Thursday and Friday off for teacher in-service days, thank goodness. I felt lousy and I couldn't afford to miss any more school. I couldn't afford to be sick either, since there was so much to do around the house. At least by Sunday we were all feeling better. Even Mom, who got up, took a shower, and got dressed. When she bounded down the stairs and into the living room, she said, "Let's go on a picnic."

"Yeah!" Chuckie clapped his chubby hands.

Michael stopped channel surfing. He looked at me. I knew what he was thinking. "That sounds good," I said to Mom, slipping a bookmark in my library book and setting it on the coffee table. "We could have it in the backyard."

"Don't be silly," Mom said. "We'll go to Cherokee Reservoir. Like we always do."

Michael's jaw dropped.

I just sat there, stunned.

Mom padded to the kitchen. We all followed. "Antonia, you go find the cooler. I'll fix us some sandwiches."

Twenty minutes later we were headed out to the car. The passenger door was a little hard to open. It might've been rusted shut, it'd been so long. While I put on Chuckie's seat belt in the backseat, Michael strapped himself in. When his eyes met mine, he smiled. Then he turned on his Gameboy.

I smiled, too. I couldn't believe we were really going. I buckled up and waited. And waited. My eyes strayed over to Mom.

Her right hand, still holding the car key in the ignition, started to shake. She released the key and gripped the steering wheel. Her knuckles turned white.

"I'm sorry," she said. "I can't do this." Her door opened and she slid out. As she walked briskly back to the house, hugging herself, Michael threw his Gameboy over the seat back and said, "I knew it."

I knew it, too. What had I been thinking?

For some unknown reason I was looking forward to Wednesday's counseling session. Maybe because I felt I was making some progress with Jazz. She seemed to open up whenever we talked about friends or family. If I could keep her on the subject, we might make a major breakthrough. Like getting past step one.

The last question on my list was "Tell me about your parents."

"What parents?" Jazz uncapped her black lipstick and spread it on thick. Then she offered it to me.

I shook my head. "I know you have parents. Quality time? Remember?"

"Oh, them," she said flatly.

"What do they do?" I asked.

"Consume." She dropped the lipstick tube in her vest pocket.

I exhaled exasperation. "You know what I mean. For a living."

"I have no idea." She batted those mascara-caked eyelashes at me. "What do yours do?"

My eyes dropped. "We're not here to talk about my parents."

"If you don't have to talk about yours, I don't have to talk about mine."

"Fine," I said. Dr. DiLeo's words came back to me: *If you share your feelings, she'll share hers.* I took a long breath. "Okay. My father is a roofer. At least, he was."

"That's cool," she said. "He serves the needs of the people. That has redeeming social value. What do you mean, he wa—" She stopped.

This was dangerous ground. I had to change the focus. "What about your mother?" I said quickly. "Does she work?"

"Uh, yeah," Jazz replied. "She works at making my life a living hell."

It was useless. She was never going to open up to me. I closed my folder.

Jazz said, "I hate my mother. In case you haven't guessed."

My eyes met hers.

"Don't look so shocked," she said. "The feeling's mutual." She climbed onto the table and assumed the lotus position. "Ohmmm," she droned. "I suppose your mother's perfect, like you."

A short laugh escaped my lips.

Jazz stopped *ohm*ing.

I stared over her head. "I don't want to talk about my mother."

Jazz's eyes narrowed. "I keep trying to find things to talk about, but you keep changing the subject." She sounded mad.

"Me?" My spine fused. "You're the one who doesn't stay on the subject."

We both turned away. The air between us charged with electricity. Finally Jazz said, "I'm sorry. I'm just in a crappy mood." She unwound from her lotus and sprawled lengthwise across the table. "My mom and I had another fight this morning. She wouldn't let me out of the house until I changed."

"Into that?" I blurted. She was wearing biker shorts, a halter top under the vest, and skull-and-crossbones earrings.

Jazz clucked. "I changed at Ram's." She rolled over onto her side and propped her head up on an elbow. "She can't accept who I am."

I said, "Maybe she just wants you to be more . . ." I couldn't say what I was thinking, which was "normal."

"Like Janey?" Jazz finished. "I'm not Janey. I'm not perfect or special, okay?"

Her voice sounded shaky and I saw tears in her eyes. For real. She hid her head and rolled onto her stomach. I didn't know what to say. What do you say when someone's about to experience an emotional breakdown? I wasn't trained for this.

But she didn't break. She murmured, "Sometimes I wish I *was* more like Janey. Or you."

"No, you don't," I said.

She lifted her head long enough to lock eyes.

I added, "If you were me, you'd die before you'd ever be seen in public in that outfit."

Jazz snorted. "Jealous, huh?"

"You know it," I said.

She turned over and sat up, cross-legged. "Maybe it's not us. Maybe it's our mothers. You want to trade?"

I rolled my eyes. "You don't want mine."

She arched an eyebrow. "You hate yours, too?"

"Yes. I mean, no." My head dropped. "Yes."

"Why, what's she like?" Jazz slid over closer to me. "Tell me, is she a bitch?"

"I . . . she . . ." My throat constricted. Quickly I gathered my stuff to leave. "I'm sorry. I can't talk about this."

Jazz ambushed me at the door. "Hey, Tone, I didn't mean—"

"I know." I cut her off. "It's just that—" The bell rang and we both jumped. Already? I checked my watch. Shouldering my book bag, I charged out the door. At the end of the hall, I glanced back to see Jazz standing stock-still, staring at me.

Can you look forward to something and dread it at the same time? That's how I felt about Friday's session. It was sort of fun meeting with Jazz. It took my mind off . . . other things. At the same time I worried that we might pick up where we left off Wednesday. With mothers.

My stomach roiled all morning just thinking about it. I had to take control. It was time to move on to step two: Restate the problem. Reflect it back to the person to make sure you understand. Jazz had told me her problem. She hated her mother. I could understand that.

She was already there, in her chair, earplugs attached. Her fingers flew up and down the tabletop. It looked weird, as if her hands were possessed. She must've sensed my presence because she glanced up and freaked.

"Are you having a seizure?" I said. "Should I call 911?"

She grinned. Dropping the CD player in one jacket pocket, she removed something else from the other and held it out to me.

"What's this?" I took it.

"A cell phone. Duh."

A cell phone? I'd never even held a cell phone. It was so light, so small. So warm from her body heat.

In answer to my unspoken question, Jazz said, "My mother calls me about six times a day to check up on me. She says we need to stay connected." Her lip curled.

I handed back the phone.

"Keep it," Jazz said.

"Oh, right. And what do I say if your mother calls?"

"Tell her I'm not in. Better yet, tell her I'm busy shooting up."

I snickered and slid the phone across the table to her. Reluctantly she pocketed it.

I said, "Let's begin by—"

"What's the one thing in your life you most regret, Tone?" she asked, cutting me off.

That was a weird question. For some reason I had an instant answer. "That I never learned to swim." Where had that come from? I hadn't thought about swimming since the summer before sixth grade when I was all hyped to spend two weeks at swim camp with Tamra. I couldn't go, of course. Mom was sick again and needed me to take care of Chuckie. Tamra. That was it. She'd been on my mind lately.

Jazz stared at me.

I shrugged. "I always thought I should know how to swim in case one of my brothers fell into a lake or something."

Jazz made a face. "What lake? We're like fifty miles from the nearest reservoir."

I felt stupid.

Jazz said, "Why don't you come over to my house tomorrow and I'll teach you how to swim?"

I scoffed. "Where? We're like fifty miles from the nearest reservoir."

"I have a pool."

My eyes sprang out of their sockets, I'm sure. "In your backyard, you mean?"

"No, in the kitchen."

Was she kidding? I held up two fingers, questioning.

She widened her eyes at me. "It's an indoor pool. Olympic-size. Plus," she hurried on, "I'm a certified Red Cross lifeguard. That's what I do in the summer, play lifeguard at my parents' country club. You tell anyone and you're dead meat." She threatened me with a fist.

"I won't." I wasn't sure I believed it anyway. My mind reeled. More than anything, I wanted to believe. I wanted to learn how to swim. I wanted to go to Jazz's house and see if she had an indoor Olympic-size swimming pool. "I can't. I have to watch my brothers. I have . . . responsibilities."

"Be irresponsible for once. Or bring your brothers along."

"Could I?"

"What? Be irresponsible or bring your brothers along?"

There was a sharp rap on the door and we both jumped. The door opened. "What are you doing in here?" an angry voice demanded. A familiar voice.

Jazz's eyes went cold. "We're doing a drug deal," she said. "What'd you think?"

I whipped my head around. "Mrs. Bartoli. Hi."

"Oh, hello, Antonia." She looked from me to Jazz and back again. "Are you using this room? I have a meeting scheduled for after school and I need to set up the VCR."

"The room's reserved," Jazz said. "Come back later."

"Jazz." I widened my eyes at her. "It's okay, Mrs. Bartoli. We're done."

I stood to leave. Jazz huffed, but followed me out. She

and Mrs. Bartoli exchanged a look. Sheer revulsion. It was so palpable, you could almost taste the venom. "You're such a suck-up," Jazz said as she caught up to me at the end of the hall. Before I could protest, she handed me a piece of notebook paper.

"What's this?" It was a row of numbers scrawled in lipstick.

Jazz recapped the lipstick tube. "My number," she said. "Call me tonight and I'll give you directions to the Luther family estate."

I slipped into Mom's room after school and shut the door. "How are you feeling, Mom?" I asked softly, perching on the edge of the bed.

"Not so good," she said. She rolled over and curled into a ball.

Do it, an inner voice commanded. "Mom, a friend asked if I could come over tomorrow. She said I could bring Chuckie and Michael, too."

I heard her sniff once, then her shoulders began to shake. When she sobbed like this, I didn't know what to do. She hated it if I touched her, so I left, closing the door behind me. No way could I leave her. So much for irresponsible.

Chapter 10

The next morning I dragged down to make breakfast, as usual. Shock. Mom was already in the kitchen. "Hello, honey." She smiled at me. "What time are you going to your friend's house?"

My chin hit the linoleum, I'm sure.

Mom added, "Don't worry about Chuckie and Michael. I'm here. I thought we'd walk to the playground or something."

My heart leapt. A whole Saturday all to myself? Without thinking, I threw my arms around Mom and squeezed. She shrank back, but didn't disintegrate.

I rushed to the telephone and called Jazz. After I told her the good news, I thought of something. "Wait, I can't."

"Why not?" Jazz said.

"I don't have a bathing suit."

"No problem," she said. "I have tons of suits." She gave me the directions to her house and I figured out the bus route. For once I was glad Mom was scared to drive, because she collected all the bus maps. I wrote down Jazz's address and phone number to leave with her. Just in case.

At the front door Mom wrapped her robe tighter and said, "Don't be too late."

"I won't." Please, God, I prayed, make her be okay. All-day okay. "I'll be home by dinner. I promise."

The number twelve bus screeched to the curb and I climbed on. The backseat was empty. A good omen. As the bus rumbled away, I didn't even look back. Just forward, down the aisle and out the front window. Even though I had brought along an algebra assignment, I didn't get it out. And for the first time ever the diesel fumes didn't make me gag.

Three blocks from home at Sinclair Boulevard a traffic jam slowed our progress. What's going on? I wondered. I peered out the dingy side window and did a double take. Overnight, a new strip mall had risen from the old landfill. Where had I been? I rode the number twelve at least twice a month to take Chuckie to the library for storytime. Was I asleep the whole way? No, usually I worked on homework or zoned out while Chuckie played with his race cars on the seat. Another thing struck me: the streets were wet.

I vaguely remembered asking Michael the night before why his socks were soaked, and his telling me his shoes had holes in them. He must've walked home in the rain.

Instead of worrying about his getting a chill on top of the flu, I'd yelled about the socks. Oh, man.

It'd be pretty muddy at the playground, I thought. But the boys wouldn't mind. They'd have a blast. Of course, I'd probably end up doing three loads of laundry.

My head lolled back against the seat. Sometimes I wished they would all disappear. Then I felt guilty for wishing it. Soon enough I'd leave for college. Three years from now, if I got into the accelerated program. Three years, if my savings lasted. Three years. It seemed like a lifetime. After I left, who'd take care of the boys? The guilt gushed back.

"Stop it!" I ordered out loud. "They're not your responsibility."

Everyone in the bus twisted around to look at me.

I slid down in my seat, feigning invisibility.

Anyway, I didn't want to think about that. I didn't have to. Not today. Today I imagined myself in another time, another place. As Princess Antonia who lived in a palace. Just like the one on the corner.

The bus screeched to a stop. My eyes strayed from the palace to the address Jazz had written down. Hey, this was it, the Luther estate. Hastily I gathered my things and jumped off the bus.

Jazz wasn't kidding. Or was she? It'd be just like her to make up some fake address, then howl hysterically with her punker pals about how she'd duped a ya-ya. I almost got back on the bus. Then something told me not to. To trust.

There was a buzzer outside the gate. As soon as I

pushed it, the house's enormous front door swung open. Jazz skipped down the driveway and flung wide the wrought-iron gate. *"Entrez,"* she said, making a swooping gesture with her arm. "Let's party, girl."

Jazz wasn't kidding either when she said she had tons of bathing suits. There were at least a dozen in her drawer, all different styles. "Try this bikini," she said, looping a teeny-tiny bra over her pinkie.

"I don't think so." Instinctively my arms encircled my body, warding off the imagined chill. "Don't you have a one-piece?"

"My lifesaving suits." She pulled out another stack from a different drawer. "Blue, red, or green?"

"Uh, green."

She tossed it to me. While I tried on the suit behind a Japanese screen in her bedroom, Jazz answered her ringing telephone. "No, not today," she said. "I have company." There was a pause. "None of your business, bat breath. Are you jealous?" she asked. Then she laughed. "Good." The springs on her round bed squeaked as she flounced around.

Her bedroom was gigantic. And gorgeous. The walls were papered with Japanese flowers, and there were closets everywhere. Walk-in. Plus mirrors, floor to ceiling. The only mirror I had was the cloudy one over my dresser, and I had to jump on the bed to see my bottom half.

Jazz hung up as I slipped out shyly from behind the screen. "Girl," she said. "You make me sick."

I tensed. "Why?"

"You are so tall and skinny. I'm like totally, insanely jealous. You could be a supermodel."

I scoffed, "Yeah, right. So, where're your parents?"

Jazz grabbed a bikini and slipped around the screen. "Mommy dearest is at an art gallery opening, but she'll be home around noon to rag on us. Papa is at the club. Playing racquetball or something else without meaning or value." She walked out. "What? What are you staring at?"

I quickly dropped my eyes. "I just never thought you were, you know, rich."

"Yeah. It's a drag."

A sarcastic laugh escaped from my lips.

"Really, I mean it. My parents are like, 'We have to be proper. We must impress. Dress for dinnah. Sip your tea, dahling.'" She stuck out a pinkie. "It's sickening."

I could handle it, I thought.

"Well, come on." Jazz yanked me by the wrist. "It's time you learned how to sink or swim."

Sink or swim. Why did that scare me?

Because swimming was scary, that's why. Especially in the indoor, Olympic-size pool that we had all to ourselves. If we somehow got to the center, we'd never find our way out. At the deep end, Jazz dived in headfirst. I sat on the edge near the shallow end and swished my legs through the water. Goosebumps prickled my skin.

Jazz stroked up to me. She stood and whipped her hair back off her face. "First, you need to lose your fear," she said.

How'd she know? My trembling lips? My ghostly pallor? Okay. I plunged in. And shriveled to a raisin.

"Lie down," Jazz said.

I looked at her like she was the psychopath I'd always suspected.

"I'll hold you up."

She wasn't displaying two fingers, unless they were hidden behind her back. I took a deep breath and fell over backward. Jazz held me while I floated. It was great. She even let me go and I stayed afloat. Then she showed me how to tread water. Pretty soon I was doing it myself. Treading water and falling into a back float. Jazz was a good teacher.

We clung to the side and I practiced breathing. Once I forgot where we were in the breathing pattern—in, out, in, out—and swallowed a gallon of chlorine. I couldn't stop coughing.

Jazz slapped me on the back. "We better take a break," she said.

"No!" I choked and regained my breath. Tried to. "I'm okay. Let's keep going."

"God, you're obsessed," she said.

I was, too. It was as if my life depended on today. On learning how to swim.

"Okay," Jazz said. "Let's take it out. Put everything together."

Sink or swim kept running through my head. *Sink or swim. Sink or* . . . suddenly everything went black.

Chapter 11

"Breathe deeply." Jazz sat on her haunches over me, rubbing my legs. "Again. That's good. Relax."

"What happened?" My voice sounded harsh. My throat felt raw.

"You blacked out. You started sinking and I had to save you." Jazz turned away and hacked.

I inhaled and exhaled. "Sorry."

She hacked again. She flopped back alongside me on the tile and said, "Good thing you are skinny. Otherwise they'd be scraping you off the bottom of the deep end. And me, too."

The skylights blurred as my eyes closed against the stinging.

"You can thank me for saving your life now," Jazz said.

But I couldn't. I couldn't say a word. A lump clogged my throat. Luckily, the sliding door opened and a cheery voice said, "There you are. Oh." The voice changed. "You didn't tell me you were having company over."

"I'm having company over," Jazz said flatly.

The woman sighed. "Hello, I'm Jasmine's mother," she said. "Marguerite Luther." She stood over me, lips pursed, forcing a smile.

Awkwardly I clambered to my feet. Still feeling dizzy, I stuck out my hand to shake. "I'm Antonia Dillon. Thank you for having me over. You have a lovely house, and a lovely pool." I glanced down at Jazz, now sprawled out on the tile. "And a, uh, lovely daughter."

Mrs. Luther's smile warmed. "And you have lovely manners." To Jazz she said, "Your taste in friends is improving."

Jazz sniped, "She's not my friend. We're in peer counseling."

I felt like crawling into the drain.

Jazz met my eyes, then looked away. "I'm teaching Tone to drown with dignity." She rolled over and, cupping both hands around her mouth, called to the empty pool, "Hey, girl. You drowning out there?" Her voice changed to mock me. "Why, yes, thank you. It's quite lovely."

Jazz's mother scorched her with a look. Pivoting on her high heels, Mrs. Luther clicked off across the tile toward the sliding glass doors. Over her shoulder she said, "Please don't pollute the pool with any more dead bodies, darling. I just had it cleaned from the last time." She exited.

"Mother thinks she's funny." Jazz got up and tossed me a towel. "Next week we'll concentrate more on putting everything together—without the sinking part."

Next week? I might not be able to come next week. "Could you show me now?"

Jazz widened her eyes at me. "You're crazy."

I shrugged. "Sink or swim."

She shook her head, but consented to another lesson. Afterward, as we headed to her room to change, Jazz said, "You look like a prune."

"So do you," I replied. "Is there such a thing as a punk prune?"

Jazz laughed. "If I'm a punk prune, you're a priss prune."

I laughed. So did she.

"You two must be famished." Mrs. Luther met us on the stair landing. "You're welcome to ask Antonia to have dinner with us, Jasmine. Your father's meeting us downtown at Gabriel's at six. We could drop Antonia off at her house afterward." She smiled at me.

Jazz sighed. I knew that sigh. She was sick of me.

She didn't have to worry. "Thank you, but I can't," I told Mrs. Luther. "I promised my mom I'd be back by dinner."

"Oh. All right." She sounded disappointed. On her way past, she squeezed my shoulder. A tingle lingered.

As Jazz flung open her bedroom door and tossed her wet towel on the bed, she said, "See? Isn't she awful?"

Awful? She seemed awesome to me. Jazz didn't know what awful was.

After changing, we went back downstairs. Mrs. Luther

cornered us in the living room. "I can't let you wait for the bus in this weather," she told me.

My gaze strayed to the front picture window, where a storm spattered frozen rain against the glass. Mrs. Luther added, "You'll catch your death of cold, especially with wet hair." She jangled her keys. "Where do you live, Antonia? I'll drop you off."

No, you can't! I screamed inwardly. "Clear on the other side of town," I said. "It's way out of your way."

"Nonsense. We'll just leave a little early and take a detour."

Before I could object, she was gone. Jazz said, "She's made up her mind. End of discussion."

Beginning of nightmare, I thought.

On the ride through town in her brand-new BMW, Jazz's mother weaved in and out of traffic and cursed drivers. She had a real bad case of road rage. So what? I thought. At least she drives. The classical music playing on the CD was soothing. When Mrs. Luther hummed along with it, the sound was sort of hypnotic. After a while, I zoned out.

Okay, I reasoned to myself, what could go wrong? Maybe in the dark, through sheets of sleet, Jazz wouldn't see where I lived. Compared to her palatial mansion, my house was slave quarters.

When I tuned back in, Jazz and her mom were having an argument. "Couldn't you at least wear something without holes?" Mrs. Luther peered in the rearview mirror at Jazz in the backseat. "You have an entire closet full of new designer dresses and suits. I wouldn't even mind if you wore the Levis you bought last week."

"I am wearing them," Jazz said.

Her mother gasped. "You mean you cut out the knees?"

"And the butt."

I twisted around from the front seat to stare at Jazz. She grinned back at me. She'd taken care to cake on the black mascara extra thick.

The heat from Mrs. Luther's white knuckles radiated through her leather gloves. Her hands clutched the steering wheel tighter.

As we got close to my house, I noticed for the first time how the gate was busted and the screen door hung by one hinge. "Here," I said quickly. "You can let me off here." At least Mrs. Marsh's house was newly painted.

I reached for the door handle, then hesitated. Something was wrong. It wasn't the peeling paint or the sagging porch. Our house was dark as death.

Chapter 12

Not even the TV flickered through the front window. Which was strange. Michael always had the TV on at night. No lights illuminated windows upstairs. The house looked abandoned.

Unfortunately, except for the porch light, Mrs. Marsh's house was dark, too.

"It doesn't look like anyone's home," Jazz's mom said.

Jazz muttered, "Duh."

"Th-that's okay," I replied. "They probably went out to eat." Which was possible, since the car was gone. The car was gone? I freaked.

Mrs. Luther said, "Antonia, I don't feel comfortable leaving you here alone, especially if your family's out for the evening. Why don't you just come eat with us? We can call your parents from the restaurant to let them know where you are. I'm sure they'll be back by the time we finish. Then I can meet them."

My blood froze. No way. Never. Not in this life. I smiled at Mrs. Luther. "Okay. Do you mind if I change first? I still feel kind of wet."

"No, not at all."

I yanked on the door handle. From the back Jazz said, "I'll go with you."

"No!" It came out a harsh bark, which made Jazz flinch. "It won't take a minute. I'll be right back."

How could I hide the fact that my house was next door now? If I ran around back . . . Oh, forget it, I thought. It's pouring rain. Maybe they'll start fighting again and forget to notice.

Racing to the door, I remembered I didn't take a house key. The sleet running down my hair and neck made me shiver. Luckily the front door wasn't locked. Which made me shiver again, this time from panic.

"Michael?" I called. "Mom? Chuckie?"

Silence. I flicked on the hall light and raced through the downstairs. Nothing. No one. I sprinted up the stairs to the bedrooms. Empty. At least they hadn't been murdered in their beds.

"Stop it," I commanded myself. "They just went out to dinner." I could hope.

In my room, I stripped to my underwear and pulled on a skirt and sweater. Hastily I brushed my damp hair back into a ponytail.

"Michael?" I called again on the way down, don't ask me

why. The house smelled funny. Like mold and garbage and cigarettes. I vowed, closing the front door behind me, that tomorrow I'd dedicate the day to housecleaning. If tomorrow ever came.

"Is your father in design graphics?" Mr. Luther asked me. He and Mrs. Luther sat across the table from Jazz and me. "I know a Tony Dillon at Omega Arts."

"No, sir," I said. "He's a . . . a . . ." How could I say *roofer?* Mr. Luther was so dressed up, so elegant. So rich. I coughed and sipped my iced tea, stalling.

Jazz yelled, "Hey, waiter dude. I need some ketchup."

Her father scowled at her.

"What?"

He sighed wearily. Thankfully it distracted him, and he sawed off a hunk of prime rib. It made my mouth water just to watch him chew. He smiled. I smiled.

"Eat." Jazz elbowed me. "Don't let your lobster get cold."

I poked my fork into the lobster tail and tore off a chunk. Copying Jazz, I dipped it in the little cup of butter. The lobster melted in my mouth. "Mmmm . . ." My eyes closed involuntarily. It tasted so good.

Jazz elbowed me again. I still felt guilty about ordering the most expensive thing on the menu, but it didn't faze Jazz. She even got fries and a chocolate shake on the side.

"Does your mother work?" Mrs. Luther asked.

The lobster lodged in my throat. I nodded. "She's a, uh . . ."—I swallowed—"image consultant." I didn't add, When she can get out of bed.

"Really?" Mrs. Luther's eyes lit up. "Does she do colors?

I've been thinking about having my colors done again. Maybe I could ask your mother—"

I coughed again. Jazz slapped me on the back. It dislodged the lobster, but not the fear. In a faint voice I replied, "She's taking some time off right now. Until my little brother starts school."

"Geez," Jazz grumbled. "Stop giving Tone the third degree, will ya? Let her eat."

I smiled up weakly, silently thanking Jazz.

"It's just that she's such a pleasure to talk to," Mrs. Luther said. "Laurent," she addressed her husband, "do you know Antonia actually changed clothes for dinner? She said she wanted to dress appropriately."

I didn't remember saying that. Maybe it was true. Or maybe I wanted an excuse to go inside and see if my family had been murdered.

"You look very nice," Mr. Luther said.

My cheeks burned. "Thank you, sir."

"She has such nice manners. Doesn't she have nice manners, Laurent? You could learn something from Antonia, Jazz."

Now I felt like crawling under the table.

Jazz muttered, "I changed for dinner, too. In case you hadn't noticed."

They both stared at her. Then, as if there'd been a temporary time warp, they turned to each other. "Constance acquired an original Howell for the gallery opening," Mrs. Luther told her husband. "She's extending the Native American exhibit through May."

Jazz smirked at me. Under her breath she said, "Don't you just love them? Aren't they just precious?"

My house was still dark when we pulled up a little after nine. No one had answered the phone the several times I'd called from the restaurant, so I wasn't surprised. "Maybe we should come in and wait with you," Jazz's mother said.

"Oh, no." No no no. "I'm sure they'll be back any minute." I tried to sound reassuring. To all of us.

"Is there someone you could call to come stay with you?"

"Mother," Jazz sighed heavily. "She's not a baby. Believe it or not, most parents trust their children enough to leave them alone in the house for a few hours."

Mrs. Luther sighed heavily. "It's not that we don't trust you, Jazz. We don't want you to be one of those horrible latchkey—" She stopped. Her eyes met mine.

"Usually Mom's home when I get here," I said.

Mrs. Luther exhaled relief. But Jazz muttered, "Saved your butt, huh, Mom?"

"It's okay if I'm alone, Mrs. Luther," I added. "Really." I opened the car door.

"I don't know—"

"Maybe she left me a message," I cut in. "Yes, I'm sure she did. I probably just missed it, since I was in such a hurry. I'll go check." I slid out and raced for the door. The sleet had stopped; now it was icicle cold. Or maybe that was me.

On the way to the kitchen I flicked on all the lights. A minute later I ran back out to the curb. The passenger side window scrolled down electrically. Jazz had moved to the front bucket seat. Holding up a folded sheet of paper, I leaned in and said, "I did miss it. It must've fallen off the fridge. They went to a double feature at the new mall." I thumbed up the street. "They should be home any minute."

Mrs. Luther hesitated. "All right, Antonia," she finally said. "You seem like a responsible person."

Jazz clucked. "Compared to me, she means."

Her mother added, "You call me if they're not home by ten."

I thanked her again for dinner. I thanked Jazz for the swim lesson.

"Yeah, no sweat," she said. As the window scrolled up, Jazz eyed the note in my hand, then looked back at me. She held my eyes.

She knows, I thought. She knows the paper is blank.

Chapter 13

I sat by the phone, waiting. What else could I do? Call the police? Call 911? Sure, and say what? My family is missing?

The clock ticked and ticked. It got later and later, darker and darker. Every time the refrigerator kicked on, I freaked.

"Okay, Antonia. Think this through," I said aloud. "Let's say she finally got up the nerve to drive again. Where would she take two little kids on a Saturday night?"

There were tons of possibilities. The movies—why not? Because we didn't go to the movies. Crowds made Mom nervous. How about the rec center? No, it closed at eight-thirty. For a drive? My stomach clenched. At night? Off a cliff?

My head fell into my hands. "Please, God," I whispered. "Please make them be okay." Just then the phone rang.

I snatched up the receiver. "Hello?"

There was a heavy silence. Then a weak voice said, "Antonia? Could you come and get us?"

"Michael!" My heart crashed through the floor. "Where are you? Are you all right? Where's Mom? Is Chuckie with you?"

Michael sniffled.

"Okay," I said more calmly. "Just tell me where you are."

"I don't know." He sniffled again. "In a hotel."

"What hotel? Where?"

"I don't know!" he shouted.

"Okay, take it easy. Is Mom there?"

Michael paused. "She can't come to the phone."

A vision materialized in my head. A crashed car. A woman lying in a pool of blood. It made me shudder, and I banished it. "Can you see the name anywhere? Is it on the phone or the door? Is there any writing paper with the hotel's name on it? Look around, Michael."

He said, "I'm not in the room. I snuck out."

A siren blared in the background, then a roar. A close one. Airplanes, I thought. He must be in a phone booth by the airport. "Is there a neon sign anywhere by the hotel? There must be something. Look." I didn't mean to sound frantic.

"I can't read it," Michael said in a tiny voice. "I don't know the words."

"Well, spell it."

He spelled, "W-y-f-a-e-r-i-n."

I wrote it down. Sounded it out. Something like Wayfair Inn. "What else do you see?"

"A bar across the street. We stopped there. Me and Chuckie stayed in the car."

A bar? "Can you read the bar's name?"

"No."

Great, I thought.

"But I remember it," he added. "Lucky Lady Saloon. Mom said, 'Lucky lady, that's me.' And she went inside."

My heart sank again, this time with a thud. "Good, Michael. Okay. I think I can find you. Is there a number on that phone?"

He read me the number. I had to ask. "Is Chuckie okay?"

"Yeah," Michael said. "He's asleep."

He'll be scared to death if he wakes up in a strange place, I thought. "Go stay with him," I told Michael. "And Mom, too. Take care of them until I get there."

"Antonia?" The weak, wavery voice returned.

"Yeah?"

"Mom's sick."

My throat constricted. "I know. Don't worry. Everything's going to be fine."

Michael inhaled a long breath. "I don't think so," he said.

There was no Wayfair Inn in the phone book, only a Wayfarer, but it was near the airport. The Lucky Lady Saloon. I looked it up, too, and confirmed the location. How did they get clear out to the airport? And why? Where was she going? Why would she stop at a bar? She didn't drink. At least, not a lot. Sometimes she used to go out for a beer after work with her girlfriends. But that was a long time ago. I wasn't even sure she had girlfriends anymore. I unfolded the bus map. "Oh, man," I thought aloud, "it'll take me hours to get there. I'll have to transfer twice." Dad never let us ride the bus at night. He said the crazies came out at night. The homeless, the winos, the thugs.

"Like you care," I muttered. "Why aren't you here to help?" Then I lost it. Waving the bus map at the ceiling, I screamed, "It's all your fault! If you hadn't gone and—"

The phone rang. I lunged for it. "Hello?"

A familiar voice said, "Tone? Hi, it's Jazz."

"Oh," I said dully.

"Mom made me call. Did your mother get home?" she asked.

My head reeled. If I lied and said yes, she might not believe me. She might ask to speak with Mom. Mrs. Luther would, for sure. Then I'd have to lie again. So many lies. I hated lying. I was already going to hell for leaving Michael and Chuckie alone today, so what difference did it make?

It made a difference. I didn't want to lie to Jazz. I was her peer counselor.

"Antonia?"

"Do you know anyone who drives?" I asked her.

She thought for a minute. "Yeah."

"Great. I need a ride somewhere."

Chapter 14

The BMW pulled up to the curb fifteen minutes later. I felt betrayed. When Jazz got out to let me in up front, I snarled at her, "I didn't mean your mother."

Jazz glared at me. "My Corvette's in the shop."

"So, where are we off to?" Mrs. Luther asked cheerfully.

I slid in and gave her the address I'd copied from the phone book. As we headed toward the highway, my breath got shorter and shorter. My whole body shook. Even though the heater was blasting, I pulled my jacket tight around me.

Mrs. Luther chattered at me over the CD player. After a while, after I didn't answer her a couple of times, I guess she gave up. Jazz just stared at me from the backseat. I could feel her eyes drilling black holes in my head.

My stomach felt queasy. If that lobster dinner hadn't cost forty dollars, I would've upchucked on the leather seat. No kidding. What was going to happen when we got to the hotel? Discovery. Disaster. Everything was going to come crashing down. I bit my trembling lip. A gush of salty blood trickled over my tongue.

"And Jazz plays the piano. Did you tell Antonia about your music?"

Jazz said, "Yeah, when I introduced myself. I said, 'I'm Jazz Luther. You know, the famous pianist.' "

Her mother ignored her. "She plays beautifully. Her teacher says she has the talent to attend Juilliard. But Jasmine refuses to compete or give a public recital."

"No, I don't," Jazz said. "You won't let me."

Jazz played the piano? That got my attention. I tried to envision her at the keys, playing a recital, going to Juilliard. The image wouldn't stick.

Mrs. Luther went on, "She's going to have to act more mature if she ever plans to audition for Juilliard."

Jazz clucked. "Who says I do?"

Listening to them bicker was better than the war raging inside my head.

The flickering neon sign was exactly as Michael had described it. The *A* and *Y* were burned out. It wasn't a hotel, though. Just a rundown, sleazy motel off the highway ramp. I'd forgotten to ask Michael what room. It didn't matter. He was huddling outside one of the red doors.

I took a deep breath. "You can just pull in over there." I pointed. "By that kid."

Mrs. Luther whipped the Beamer into one of the dozen empty spaces and turned off the ignition.

"You don't have to come in," I told her, lifting the door handle.

"Nonsense," she said.

"No—"

But she was already out of the car and heading toward the room. Jazz scurried out behind her.

Michael scrambled to his feet when he saw us. "This is my brother Michael," I introduced them.

Mrs. Luther reached out a gloved hand. His scared eyes met mine. I didn't know what to do either, so I nodded okay. He shook the hand limply. She said, "We've come to help."

Then go away, I thought. Get in that Beamer and drive back to paradise. Leave us alone here in hell.

"How's . . . everyone?" I asked Michael.

He caught my drift. "Not good."

"Why don't we go inside out of the cold?" Mrs. Luther suggested.

Michael met my eyes. His sick expression mirrored my feeling of foreboding.

Mrs. Luther opened the door.

Chuckie lay curled in a ball on the single bed, his thumb in his mouth. "That's my other brother, Chuckie," I said quietly. "Let's just get him and go."

"Where's your mother?" Jazz asked.

I shot eye-daggers at Jazz. She didn't flinch, just continued to hold my gaze. Then she blinked off and looked at

Michael. His eyes strayed to the corner. Don't look, I pleaded silently.

But she did.

There, behind the TV, sat Mom. She was hunched up, hugging her knees on the filthy floor. "Mrs. Dillon?" Jazz's mom said softly.

A sort of whimper rose from Mom's throat. A wounded-animal sound. Mrs. Luther approached and knelt down in front of Mom. She touched her shoulder. "What's your mother's name, Antonia?" she asked without taking her eyes off Mom.

"Patrice," I replied.

"Patrice. I'm a friend, Patrice. Can you hear me?"

Mom whimpered and scrunched up tighter. I walked over and pulled Mom's dress down over her knees so you couldn't see . . . you know. "She gets like this sometimes," I said. "When she doesn't take her medicine."

"Medicine? What kind of medicine?" Mrs. Luther stood up suddenly.

I stepped back. "I don't know. Something for her nerves."

"Oh." Mrs. Luther frowned. "Do you know her doctor's name?"

"No," I said. "I'm sorry." My voice caught.

"All right." Mrs. Luther removed her gloves and stuck them in her purse. "I'm going to the motel office to make a few phone calls. Antonia, Jazz, you get Chuckie and Michael into the car." She handed Jazz the keys. "I'll be back to help with your mother," she said to me. Her hand grasped mine and squeezed. "Don't worry, Antonia. Everything's under control. Everything's going to be fine."

Fine, I thought. Whose definition?

After she left, Michael grabbed my coat sleeve. "Why'd you bring her?" he snarled. "She's going to ruin everything."

I stared at the motel door. He was right. But for some reason, I felt relieved.

Jazz said, "Don't worry, Michael." Her words didn't convey much comfort, especially when she added, "My mother's a control freak. Believe her when she says everything's under control."

"Where are we going?" Michael asked as soon as we were all bundled in the car and driving away. Mom was strapped in up front next to Mrs. Luther, while the four of us crammed together in back. Chuckie lay in my lap, sucking away on his thumb. Out the window, I watched the wavering Wayfarer sign slowly disappear in the distance. "Are you taking us to the cops?" Michael asked.

Mrs. Luther glanced back at him. She smiled. "Of course not, sweetie. Why would I do that? You haven't done anything wrong."

I could tell he didn't believe her. He scootched closer to the side window, scrunching up his shoulders.

"Where *are* we going, Mom?" Jazz asked.

Her mother exhaled. "Home. You're all coming over to spend the night with us. Won't that be fun?" She winked at us in the rearview mirror.

Jazz smiled at me like, See? Control freak.

Leaning around Jazz, I said to Michael, "They have an indoor swimming pool."

He shrugged.

"And a game room," Jazz added. "With a big-screen TV. We have all the Disney movies."

That perked him up.

She tweaked his cheek. "It'll be fun."

He jerked away.

Fun. For how long? I wondered.

We pulled into the driveway at the Luther estate. At night, with the outdoor globes illuminated and lights twinkling in the upstairs windows, the place looked like a gingerbread house. The fragrance of cinnamon even swirled through the air. Or maybe that was Mrs. Luther's sweet perfume. I opened the car door and slid out, carrying Chuckie. Jazz took Michael's hand. When Mrs. Luther didn't follow with Mom, my heart raced. "Where're you taking her?" I said.

Mrs. Luther smiled somberly. "I have a dear friend, a doctor. I called him at the motel and he said to go ahead and bring her in."

"In where?"

"St. Joseph's Hospital," she said.

I paused. "She's afraid of hospitals. Doctors, too."

"She's afraid of everything," Michael said.

I glared at him.

"Well, she is." He kicked an imaginary pebble.

Jazz's mom bent down in front of Michael. "Sometimes we're scared of things that are good for us. Like doctors and hospitals. We just need someone to help us get over our fears. Okay?"

He nodded.

I held Chuckie tighter.

"Come on." Jazz tugged on Michael's hand. "She'll be okay, guys. Trust us." She caught her mom's eye, then blinked back. "Trust me, at least."

I looked from Jazz, all black smiles, to Mrs. Luther, all red smiles, and thought, Who are you? I don't even know you people.

"By the way, Antonia," Mrs. Luther added. "Is there someone I should call? A relative? A grandparent? Sister, brother?"

Mom's sister, Aunt Hannah—but she and Mom didn't get along. Besides, she lived in Ohio. "No," I told her. "There's no one."

"How about your father?"

Jazz yanked Michael harder. "There's no one, Mom, okay? Just go."

Chapter 15

I didn't think I'd ever get to sleep, but suddenly it was morning. A vague memory resurfaced—dragging up the stairs, settling Michael and Chuckie in, falling into bed beside Jazz. Now sunlight streamed in through Jazz's window, blinding me. I propped up on my elbows and peered over the lump of flowered comforter to Jazz's digital clock. Nine-thirty-eight. Oh, no! School. Then I remembered it was Sunday.

Jazz groaned.

As quietly as possible, I took off the nightgown Jazz had loaned me, put on my sweater, and swiveled my skirt back into place. Tiptoeing out into the hallway, I slipped into my shoes and went in search of my brothers.

Mr. Luther had put them in a guest bedroom last night.

He wanted to give each of them a separate room, but I said no. Chuckie couldn't sleep alone. He woke up crying at least once every night. He had nightmares. Monsters and bogeymen were always after him. Usually it was me who got up to calm him down. Plus he had that . . . other problem. Now I felt guilty. I'd slept clear through the night. Who'd gotten up with Chuckie?

The guest room was empty. I panicked. My family was missing again. Then I heard voices downstairs. The smell of frying bacon hit my nose.

It took a while to find the kitchen, but there they were —Mr. Luther at the table with Chuckie in his lap. Michael sat across from them. "Antonia, good morning." Mr. Luther set down his fork and scooted back his chair. He stood. "Please." He waved to the table. "Have a seat. Would you like O.J. or grape juice?"

I slid into the empty chair next to Michael. He grinned at me. "I had both."

"Or both?" Mr. Luther grinned at me, too.

"Orange juice," I said. "Thank you."

Mr. Luther swung Chuckie over his head and planted him atop his shoulders. Chuckie whooped with glee. "Do you like your eggs scrambled, over easy, or sunny side up?"

I looked at Michael. "I had scrambled," he said.

"Scrambled is fine. Thank you."

Chuckie wiggled his fat fingers at me in a wave. I waved back. '"Have you heard anything about our mother?" I asked as I spread a napkin over my lap.

Mr. Luther didn't answer right away. Setting Chuckie on

the counter, he cracked two eggs into a skillet. "When Margie left her last night, your mother was resting comfortably." He smiled across the breakfast bar at me. "I'm sure Margie will have more to tell you when she gets up. Any sign of life from Jazz?"

"She was breathing," I said.

"Rats." He held up a palm. "Just kidding." He didn't smile like he was kidding.

"What's everyone doing up at the crack of dawn?" Jazz appeared in the doorway, rubbing her eyes. Her smeared black eyes. Grousing, she sank into a chair across from me.

"Good morning," her father said.

Jazz's forehead crunched the table.

"Breakfast?" he asked her as he set a heaping plate in front of me. Besides the scrambled eggs, there were three strips of bacon, a slice of ham, a blueberry muffin, and a pile of hash-brown potatoes. For a second I just stared. And drooled.

"Coffee," Jazz muttered.

Mr. Luther sighed. "Antonia, would you like coffee too?"

"Uh, sure."

Michael widened his eyes at me. I widened mine back. "Me too," he said.

Mr. Luther chuckled. He poured us all cups of coffee. With lots of cream.

"Make mine a double espresso," Mrs. Luther said. She sort of floated into the room on a breeze, her lacy blue robe billowing out behind her. "What a night." She squeezed my shoulder on her way past.

"And who is this little elf?" Mrs. Luther paused in front

of Chuckie. "I don't believe we were properly introduced." She tickled his ribs.

"I'm Chuckie," he said in a giggle.

"Nice to meet you, Chuckie." She shook his pudgy hand.

Chuckie beamed. "Nithe to meet you, too."

Taking her cup from her husband, she said, "You all have such beautiful manners. Don't they, Jasmine?" She sat down next to Jazz.

Jazz grumbled.

"Aren't you eating breakfast?" her mother asked.

Jazz made a gagging sound.

"Yes, she is." Mr. Luther set a heaping plate in front of her. She shoved it away.

"Jasmine!" he snapped. "Sit up and eat. Act like a human being. We have guests, for chris'sakes."

With a heavy sigh, Jazz straightened herself. Sighing again, she snatched the muffin off her plate and snarled, "Pass the butter. Pleeease."

Mrs. Luther turned to me. "Dr. Vargas, my doctor friend, admitted your mother to St. Joseph's last night. She was resting comfortably when I left. After she's feeling a little better, he wants to do a psychiatric workup on her."

"She's not crazy!" Michael cried.

"Of course she isn't." Mrs. Luther reached over and patted Michael's hand.

He recoiled. "She's just scared," he mumbled.

"Of course she is. And so are you."

I met Mrs. Luther's eyes and swallowed hard. "Can we see her?" I asked. My voice wavered. Hold it together, Antonia, my brain commanded.

Mrs. Luther smiled. "Give her a couple of days. Let's get her back on her feet. I'm sure she wouldn't want you to see her like this."

Like what? I wanted to say. We've been living with her like this our whole lives. Well, not our whole lives. She hadn't always been this bad.

My head sank slowly. I wondered if I'd ever see her again. And if I cared. What? I couldn't believe I was thinking that. I was such a horrible person.

"Antonia?" Mrs. Luther cocked her head at me. "What are you thinking, dear?"

"Mother, please," Jazz cut in. "You're not her psychiatrist." She made a face at me, then grinned. "I am."

I had to smile. Yeah, right.

Michael asked the question that was on my mind. "What's going to happen to us?"

"Well, now." Mrs. Luther exhaled. She took a bite of bacon. Brushing off her fingertips, she said, "We really should try to get hold of your father." She lifted her cup and arched her eyebrows at me.

I swallowed hard. "That . . . could be a problem."

"Why, dear?"

My cheeks flared. I stared blindly at my eggs.

Jazz said, "Because he's dead. God, Mother. You're so dense."

Mrs. Luther's lips grew taut. Then she turned empathetic eyes on me. "Is that true?"

Michael's eyes locked on to mine. A silent agreement passed between us.

I nodded. It wasn't, but it seemed easier than the truth.

Chapter 16

"I'm sorry I just blurted it out like that," Jazz said. We were back in her room, listening to music. At least, Jazz was. I busied myself making her bed. When she looked over at me for a response, I pretended to tuck my pillow in tighter. Jazz turned up the volume on her CD player. She'd picked out a heavy metal band, which I usually despise. Except now the crashing and bashing drowned out my thoughts. It was soothing, in a weird way. The words were so angry. "Hurt me, baby. Slash me. Burn me." I could really relate to them.

Sitting in front of her lighted vanity mirror, Jazz worked on her makeup. She twirled around on the little stool and tossed me the tube of black lipstick.

Perching on the edge of her bed behind her, I rolled the tube around in my hand.

She said, "If your mom's not working right now, how do you eat and stuff?" She gasped, covering her mouth with her hand. "You don't have a job after school, do you?"

"No," I answered, although I'd been thinking about it. "We have money." The check Mom got every month. Come to think of it, I hadn't seen the check these last couple of months. Maybe that's why Mom was using my college money. Which wouldn't last forever. "Not as much money as you," I added.

Jazz clucked and whirled back around on the stool.

I fiddled with the lipstick tube and decided not to use it. Carefully I replaced the tube on the vanity next to about a hundred others.

Jazz shot up. "C'mon, get dressed." She yanked me up off the bed.

"I am dressed."

"Then get undressed."

"What?"

"I'll give you another swimming lesson."

That seemed a worthwhile way to spend a Sunday. Better than what I usually did, which was laundry and housework and homework—"Yikes! I need to go pick up my homework."

Jazz made a face.

"I mean, so I can do it later."

She smiled and slung a swimsuit at me.

* * *

The Luthers invited us to stay again Sunday night, which was a relief since I didn't know what else we'd do. I figured there were laws against kids living alone. Even though that's essentially what we'd been doing for the last six months.

When Mrs. Luther dropped me off to get my homework, I grabbed some clean clothes for the boys. I knew Chuckie'd need extra underwear, too. I packed a couple of blouses that I could wear with my skirt, even though they needed ironing. Everything did.

Sunday afternoon, Jazz had a piano lesson. "My teacher is Gregoire St. Jacques," she told me. "Isn't that romantic?" I was still trying to picture Jazz playing the piano. "Gregoire St. Jacques," Jazz breathed. She pronounced it *San Shock*.

It was romantic.

She added, "I'd give up the piano altogether if it wasn't for Gregoire. He understands me. Like he says, 'Muzeek comes from ze heart.'" Her eyes gleamed. "You probably can't tell I'm deeply in love with Gregoire."

My eyes widened at her and she laughed. Then she threatened me with a fist. "Don't you dare tell him."

"Gregoire and I never discuss you," I said, getting out my history homework.

Jazz whapped me. The doorbell chimed and she leapt off the bed. Fluffing her hair in the vanity mirror, she rechecked her lipstick. Perfectly purple.

"You'd better stay here," Jazz said. "Gregoire doesn't allow other people around during my lesson. Not even my mother." She grinned. "Another reason why I love him."

She sprinted to the end of the hall, stopped, inhaled deeply, and sauntered casually down the stairs.

Following her instructions, I got up and closed the door. As I returned to the desk, I sighed. If I had a desk this big, I'd get my work done in half the time. If I had a desk at all . . .

I barely had time to review the introduction on pre-Columbian civilizations before the sound struck. A chord. Then a scale. Up and down, up and down. The notes swirled through the air; they beckoned me.

That, and my curiosity. What kind of person was Gregoire San Shock?

Jazz's door opened without a squeak. As I sneaked down the stairs, the trill of another scale swept up to meet me. Like a tidal wave, it swelled from the baby grand in the living room and rolled up the staircase. Even though Jazz was only warming up, the music was breathtaking.

Gregoire stood behind Jazz, conducting with his left hand as if she were an orchestra. Which, to my ears, she was. Gregoire was tall and thin. He had blond shaggy hair, which he wore in a ponytail. It didn't cover his bald spot. I only noticed the shiny circle on his head because I was hovering over him, hunched down behind the stair railing.

"Let us play the polonaise," Gregoire said in this exotic French accent.

Jazz groaned. "I hate the polonaise. Let's jam." Her fingers trilled the keys and she spun around on the piano stool.

Gregoire just looked at her.

She huffed. "God, I was just joking around."

"You do not have time to joke around. The Chopin competition is next Saturday. All three pieces must be perfect. Be serious now, Jazz. You can win this thing, you know."

"I am going to win it," she said defiantly. "I'm the best. You said so yourself."

"That was my first mistake." He grinned at her. Deep dimples dented his cheeks.

I could see why she was in love with him. I think I was, too.

"Play!" he ordered.

And she did. Gloriously. My jaw came unhinged. *Awesome* was the only word to describe her playing. She had a God-given talent. I closed my eyes to listen. It was so moving, so consuming, that I didn't notice the stirring beside me. When I opened my eyes, Michael and Chuckie had crouched down next to me.

"Wow," Michael breathed.

I nodded. That's all you could say. Chuckie just sat there, mesmerized. We were all mesmerized. We settled in on the stairs like the Three Stooges, listening to Jazz's entire piano lesson.

At the end, I hustled the boys back upstairs to the game room. Downstairs I heard Gregoire say, "The mazurka and concerto are perfect, Jazz. But the polonaise is not. It does not come from here." He fisted his heart.

Jazz looked crushed. "I'll work on it," she said. "I promise. I won't let you down."

He gathered up his things and headed for the door.

Before leaving, he turned and said, "It's not me you will be letting down." His eyes strayed up to the balustrade and met mine.

My face flared. Quickly I backed away and slipped into Jazz's room.

A minute later she tromped in. "Your mother was right," I said from the desk. "You are an extremely talented pianist."

She clenched the doorknob. "You heard me?"

"We all heard you. God in heaven heard you."

"Did She?" To the vaulted ceiling, Jazz performed a sweeping bow. "I hope You enjoyed the show." She smirked. Sprawling across the bed, she hugged a pillow to her chest and said, "So, what'd you think of Gregoire?"

"As they say in France," I replied, "ooh-la-la."

Jazz squealed and tossed the pillow at me.

I fended it off with a forearm. "What are you practicing for? A competition?"

"A young artists' Chopin competition. And a recital next month. Oh, and, Tone, do me a favor." She sat up, looking serious. "Don't tell Animal or Ram or Eeks about the piano."

I frowned. "Why not?"

She shrugged. "They'd think it was, you know." She wrinkled her nose.

"Normal?" I ventured.

"Nerdy," she countered. "I mean, classical music?" She made her psycho face. "And look at this." She rolled off the bed and hurried to the closet. Riffling through a rack of clothes, she yanked something out of the back. "*This* is what my mother expects me to wear to the Chopin competition." She held up a dress on a hanger.

I gasped. It was gorgeous. Lush blue velvet with a wide white satin sash.

"It's hideous, isn't it?" Jazz hung it back up.

I didn't say what I was thinking. Wishing, praying. That if she didn't want the dress, would she please give it to me?

Chapter 17

Monday morning Mr. Luther dropped us off at school on his way to work. "You think we could do peer counseling today?" Jazz asked, glancing back over her shoulder as her father drove away. "I might not be here on Wednesday."

"Uh, sure," I said. "Where're you going Wednesday?"

Jazz pulled out her makeup kit and began her transformation. "I might be ditching the rest of the week. I really need to practice that polonaise."

Someone called, "Yo, Jazz."

She whipped her head around. "Later," she said to me as she loped off toward the science wing.

Good, I thought. That solved one problem. I didn't really want to be seen with Jazz. People would talk. "Like who?" I muttered. "All your friends?" Still, there was my reputation to consider.

At our afternoon peer counseling session, Jazz started off by saying, "Your brothers are so sweet. It must be really fun to have them around."

"Fun?" I scoffed. "They're a pain."

"Really?"

I just looked at her. "Not Chuckie. He's okay, but Michael's a brat. A brat and a half."

She pursed her purple lips. "He does seem kind of angry."

"That's an understatement. He'd kill the world if he could."

"Why?"

I took a deep breath. "Don't ask me. I'm not a child psychologist."

"You're not?" She looked shocked. "But DiLeo said you were. I want my money back."

I sneered.

Jazz flung off her boots and climbed up onto the table. "Tell me about your mom," she said. "What happened to her?"

I folded my hands on the table and looked up at Jazz. She sat lotus style, facing me. "I have a better idea," I said. "You tell me about your mom."

She stared over my head, trancelike. "What about her? Ohmmm," she chanted.

"Why are you so mean to her?"

Jazz stopped chanting. She frowned. "I'm not."

"Yes, you are. You talk down to her and mouth off and do everything you can to deliberately make her mad."

Jazz's eyes narrowed. She straightened her spine and took up her mantra. After a minute of droning, she stopped and said, "She gets on my nerves, okay? She's always on my case. She hates my clothes, she hates my hair, she hates my friends—except you." Her eyes met mine, briefly. "She hates everything I am. Everything I do."

"Not everything," I countered. "She loves the way you play the piano."

"Yeah, and she knows if she ever pulls that trick on me and my friends again, I'll quit."

"What trick?" I asked.

Jazz answered, "She called the cops on us."

"When?" My eyes grew wide. "What'd you do?"

"Nothing!" Jazz screeched. Then realizing how loud her voice was, she took a calming breath and said, "We were just hanging out at Ram's, not doing anything. Ram was really bummed about his mom and we were trying to cheer him up. Telling jokes and stuff. I guess I lost track of time because all of a sudden the cops show up at the shed. Ram tells them to take off, so they bust in and start frisking us. Tearing the place up, looking for drugs or guns, I don't know what all. Ram says, 'I got a water pistol in my pocket.' When he reaches for it, one of the cops shoves him up against the wall and almost breaks his arm. I mean, God. This is Ram. He is the sweetest, gentlest person. He's so peaceful he won't even let us step on cockroaches in his presence. It was only like eight o'clock, but if I'm not home by dinner my mother calls out the National Guard."

"How do you know it was your mother who called?" I said.

Jazz's face hardened. "Because she was sitting in her Beamer across the street from Ram's house the whole time. Everyone saw her. It was humiliating. God." Her jaw muscles clenched. "Mother thinks my friends are corrupting me." A wicked smile spread across Jazz's face. "If she only knew."

That was pretty bad. I could see why Jazz was angry.

She said quietly, "The thing that really gets me is, she doesn't trust me. Doesn't she know me better than that?" Her eyes searched mine.

"Maybe she thinks you've changed."

"I haven't!"

"Maybe she's afraid you will."

Jazz stared. "God, you're good."

My face flared.

"Wrong, but good. All my mother wants is to control me. Just like she controls my father and my sister and everyone else in the world." With her two index fingers, Jazz formed horns on her head. "She's like the mother from hell."

I smiled. "You still want to trade?"

Jazz held my eyes for only a second before blinking away.

No, I didn't think so.

After school I waited for Jazz on the front steps outside. I didn't know what else to do. I wasn't sure if Mr. Luther was picking us up or if we were walking. If we were walking, there was no way I could find my way to Jazz's house alone.

Thankfully, she was late. Most of the crowd had dispersed by the time she appeared around the corner of the science wing. She was with her punk groupies, headed my way.

Oh, no, I thought. I'm not going with them. They looked so weird. Worse than Jazz with their spiked hair and leather jackets. Two of the girls wore shorts. At least, I assumed they had on shorts under their jackets.

Suddenly Jazz stopped. She turned toward her gang and said something. They all reversed direction and started walking away. Jazz waited until they'd disappeared around the building before loping toward me.

It gave me a strange feeling. Like she didn't want to be seen with me.

"Sorry," Jazz said. "I forgot you were staying at my house."

My gaze hit the pavement. "Jazz," I said softly. "I'm sorry about today. I didn't mean to—"

"I know," she broke in. "I'm sorry, too. Some days I'm a total bitch."

"No, you're not." I shook my head. "I'm just really grateful for everything your mom's doing for us. Both your parents. And you, too. I mean, at least we have a place to stay for . . . however long."

Jazz smiled somberly. "Hey, it's no problem. It's not like we don't have a hundred empty rooms, you know? Come on." She grabbed my sleeve and yanked me down the stairs. "The caterer's probably already set up our after-school-snack buffet out on the front forty."

She was kidding, right?

* * *

"I wonder who's here," Jazz said as we approached her front gate. It was open, and a white car was parked in the driveway. "Can't be the Clean Team. They don't come till Tuesday."

The Clean Team? "You have maid service?"

Jazz rolled her eyes at me. "You didn't think my mother performed manual labor, did you?"

My eyes dropped. I guess I did.

Jazz added in a sneer, "Mother hires all kinds of help. Cooks, gardeners, maids. It's like totally pretentious, don't you think?"

I don't know. I was thinking it'd be great.

Mrs. Luther and another lady rose from the living room sofa when we walked in. "Hello, girls," Jazz's mother said. The other lady smiled at me, then glanced at Jazz. Her face changed. I recognized the expression. The same look of revulsion that Jazz had gotten from Mrs. Bartoli, with a little fear mixed in.

The lady bustled over to Jazz and stuck out her hand. "Hello, Antonia," she said. "I'm Karen Millbrook, from Social Services."

Jazz lurched back. Mrs. Luther laughed. "No, no," she said. "That's my daughter Jasmine." She strode over to me and squeezed me around the shoulders. "This is Antonia."

The lady looked relieved. My brain told me to run, but my feet wouldn't move. Maybe because there was nowhere to run to. Nowhere to hide.

Chapter 18

She asked me to call her Karen. Like we were going to be friends or something. Like there was going to be this long-term relationship. We all sat on the sofa staring at one another. Actually, Karen was staring at me, while I tried to morph into the ceramic magnolias on the coffee table.

What was happening? How did I get here? How did we become a charity case? Why did I feel like my whole life had been one long dream? Not this life; this was a nightmare. The one before, when things were normal.

"Your mother may be in the hospital for a while, Antonia," Karen said.

That demorphed me. "How long?"

"It's hard to say," she replied. "Until she's stable. Until it's safe for her to leave."

Safe? From what? I met Karen's eyes. I knew from what. Herself.

"You know we'd love for you to stay with us," Mrs. Luther said. "But I'm afraid it's just not possible."

My heart sank. Not only were we charity cases, we were homeless, too.

Jazz said, "Why can't they stay here?"

Her mother gave her a look. It said, Keep out of this.

It was no mystery to me why she didn't want us to stay. Who needed three crummy kids to take care of in addition to a delinquent daughter?

Karen said, "And you don't have a father, is that right?"

I shook my head. Funny how lying gets easier the more you do it.

Mrs. Luther piped up, "Even though you have to go to a foster home, I insisted they place you and your brothers together."

Foster home. So that was it. The beginning of the end.

Mrs. Luther chuckled. "Michael thought you were all going to an orphanage."

"What's the difference?" I nailed Karen with the question.

Her face contorted, like she was new to destroying people's lives. "There's no comparison," she said. "In fact, we don't even have orphanages anymore. So forget all the horror stories you've heard or seen. This isn't Bosnia. You'll be placed with a very nice family."

Mrs. Luther reached over and patted my arm. "Temporarily, Antonia. It's only until your mother is better. Who knows? It might be just a couple of days."

Karen shot her a look. It clearly said, Don't get her hopes up.

Michael and Chuckie clomped down the stairs, lugging backpacks. New backpacks. Mrs. Luther rose. "I've packed a few things for you, too, Antonia." She hurried to the dining room and back. On her arm dangled an overstuffed, sporty new backpack. She held it out to me.

If I took it, it meant I was accepting charity. It meant everything I was feeling right now was real. My eyes welled with tears.

"Oh, sweetie." Mrs. Luther crushed me against her, whapping my butt with the backpack. What was in there, forty pounds of sirloin steak? She slipped the straps up over my shoulders. Make that fifty pounds.

During all of this, Jazz remained silent. She just sat and glared at her mother.

Don't blame her, I wanted to say. It isn't her fault. But I couldn't say it. I couldn't say anything.

Karen led us out to the driveway. My brothers must've felt as miserable as I did; we looked like we were heading out on the orphan train.

Our foster folks were named Mr. and Mrs. Abeyta. They stepped out onto the porch as we drove up. After Karen introduced us, we stood around looking stupid. Chuckie clung to my leg, sucking his thumb. Michael would've, too, if he hadn't been trying to act so brave.

"Call me Tillie," Mrs. Abeyta said. "And my husband here is Luis."

Luis said, "Hello, kids," and smiled.

I tried to smile back but couldn't.

"Have you had dinner?" Tillie asked.

We shook our heads in unison.

"You must be starving. I'll whip something up."

"I'll stop by tomorrow, kids," Karen said. She passed a silent message to the Abeytas, something like, They're all yours now. Do whatever you want with them. To us she said, "Everything will be fine."

The three of us watched her walk down the driveway, get into her car, and drive away. It felt as if she were taking our lives away with her.

"Come on," Tillie said, pulling open the screen door. "It's getting chilly out here."

We trailed Tillie through the house to the kitchen, like sheep led to slaughter. She sat us at the table while Luis sliced ham for sandwiches. Tillie told us she and Luis had raised eight kids. Since the last one left for college, the house was too quiet. "Feels like ghosts," she finished.

"Those are ghosts," Luis teased her. "It's the kids coming back to haunt us. We'll never get rid of 'em."

Ghosts. Just what we needed. Just what we looked like.

The sandwiches smelled delicious. Thick ham and Swiss cheese. They must've tasted good too, the way Michael and Chuckie were scarfing them down. I took one bite and couldn't swallow past the lump in my throat.

"Not hungry?" Tillie asked me.

It took every ounce of self-control I had not to start bawling.

* * *

I had my own room, which used to be the Abeytas' oldest daughter's room. Yolanda. She was married with two kids now, Tillie informed me as she set a stack of towels on the cedar chest. Yolanda had left behind her stuffed animals and books and posters. Most of the posters were these glistening guys in skimpy swimsuits, all flexing their muscles. How could I sleep with them staring at me? How could I even get undressed?

I didn't have to explain about Chuckie's nightmares because both boys were put in the room next to mine, in a bunk bed. Which they loved, I could tell. I wandered over near the door to eavesdrop. Luis told them, "Our boys collected model airplanes. See? They never finished this one. Maybe you could work on it, Michael. And, Chuckie, Tillie made up this whole basket of toys for you."

"Okay," he said cheerfully.

I wanted to charge in there, grab their arms, and scream, "Don't touch anything. We're not going to be here that long." But I didn't. And I didn't tell Tillie or Luis about Chuckie's other problem. Let them discover the wet sheets in the morning. Let them think it was their fault.

I was a terrible person. No wonder this was happening to me. Like a robot, like the ya-ya I was, I worked on my homework and went to bed.

The Abeytas' house was in our school district, thank goodness. At least we wouldn't have the added trauma of starting new schools. Tillie was retired, so she planned to stay home with Chuckie. Luis drove Michael and me to our schools, since they were on the way to his restaurant business. Or so he said. "Meet me right out front afterward," Luis told me as he pulled to the curb. "Just think of me as your own personal chauffeur." He grinned. The corners of his eyes crinkled, just like Dad's do. Did, I mean.

Don't cry, Antonia. Don't cry. Don't cry. I concentrated on my loafers crunching through the frosted grass and somehow made it through the front door intact.

The day was a haze. My body was there, but it was just going through the motions. My body was good at that. Except I made a multiplication mistake on a quadratic equation I was computing at the board. Mrs. Bartoli smiled her famous I'm-sorry-but-that-is-incorrect smile. It was the first time she'd extended it to me.

Obviously my head was somewhere else. I knew where —at home. Did anyone take the trash out? Tuesday is trash day. If the trash isn't at the curb, they won't pick it up. Did I turn off the hall light before I left? Did I make the beds? Milk! The milk in the refrigerator would go sour if we didn't drink it. Did I remember to flush the toilet after Chuckie? Did I fold the laundry? Did I . . .

The bell clanged over my head, jolting me back into automatic.

While passing between classes I felt a hand clamp over my arm. It yanked me out of the stampeding herd. "Tone, you're here."

I blinked back to the present. Today Jazz's hair was pink. Or someone had glued a glob of cotton candy onto her scalp. "Where else would I be?" I said.

"I mean, you're here in school."

"As opposed to out in the park setting small children on fire?"

She smirked.

I exhaled a long breath. The one I'd been holding all morning. "You're here, too. I thought you were going to ditch."

She shrugged. "Change in plans. So, you're still in this school?"

I nodded. "The powers that be think it'd be just too, too traumatic if we changed homes, parents, lives, and schools all on the same day."

Jazz smiled. "So I'll see you in session."

"It's only Tuesday."

"You know what they say: live for today." She nudged me in the arm and took off. "Don't be late," she called over her shoulder. "We have a lot of stuff to talk about."

The dread overwhelmed me. I really, really did not want to talk about this.

"Jazz, I really don't want to talk about it," I told her right off.

"Come on." She scooted her chair closer. "At least tell me what they're like."

"Who?"

"Duh," she said. "Your foster parents."

Foster parents. I sighed. "They're ugly, evil little gnomes who keep us locked in the root cellar with the rats. Vicious rats. Rabid rats."

One side of Jazz's lips cricked up. "Do they make you eat gruel?"

"Gallons of it." I added, "And what's worse, their dog sleeps under the table during meals and farts."

Jazz burst into laughter. After she recovered, she said, "Come on. Tell me the truth."

Leave me alone, I thought. Just let me be.

"Tone." Folding her arms, she said, "You never share anything. You're so selfish sometimes."

Selfish? That did it. I spun on her. "They're young, rich, glamorous yuppies with a four-car garage and a built-in swimming pool. Their problem is they have this self-centered, thankless daughter who doesn't give a damn about anything or anyone."

Jazz's face went white. Her eyes said murder, so I stood to go. "By the way, tell your mother thank you for all the new clothes. Tell her I don't plan to cut up a thing."

Jazz beat me to the door. "I give a damn," she said.

"Let me out," I croaked. My face felt fireball red.

"You're not supposed to run, remember?"

I wrenched open the door.

She blocked my exit with her arm. "Don't you want to know what I give a damn about?"

I just looked at her. "Not really, Jazz. You know why? Because *I* don't give a damn. Not about you. Not about anything or anyone." I broke through her arm block and fled down the hall.

She hollered after me, "I give a damn about you!"

Chapter 19

Karen was sitting at the Abeytas' kitchen table with Tillie and Chuckie when we got home from school. "Hello, kids." Tillie got up and rushed over to greet us. She hugged Michael. "How was your day?"

"Good," he said. "I had the best lunch of anybody."

Tillie beamed. Then she hugged me. "How was your day?"

Awful, I didn't say. I didn't hug back either. Guess I didn't feel very huggable.

Luis kissed Tillie on the cheek and sat down next to Chuckie. My little brother was busy gathering together his *Star Wars* action figures that the Luthers had given him. When I walked by and tousled his hair, he barely acknowledged me.

"You must be starved," Tillie said. "Sit down and have a snack."

There was a plate of chocolate chip cookies on the table. They smelled freshly baked, sweet and chocolatey. While Tillie poured each of us a glass of milk, Karen said, "Your mother's feeling a little better today. She'd like to see you."

"Yeah?" My heart leapt. "When?"

"Any time."

"Let's go." I jumped to my feet. "Come on, Michael."

His eyes stayed on the cookies. "I'm hungry," he said. "You go."

I just stared at him.

Karen got up and motioned me toward the door. "We'll bring you a report, Michael. How's that?"

"Good," he garbled, stuffing his face.

Tillie said, "Here, Antonia. Take some cookies with you."

That's a good idea, I thought. "Could I take some to Mom?"

Tillie said, "Well, sure." She stacked a dozen or so in a paper lunch sack and handed it to me. "Tell her to enjoy them."

She will, I didn't say. I should have said it, just like I should have said thank you.

As we backed down the driveway, I muttered more to myself than Karen, "I can't believe Michael."

"I can," Karen said. "He's confused and scared. He probably remembers how your mom was the last time he saw her."

"That's no excuse," I said. "He's a traitor. One lousy cookie and he sells out his own mother."

“Oh, come on. He’s not strong as you, Antonia.” Karen looked at me. “Not many people are.”

I turned away. I didn’t feel strong. I felt weak and helpless.

The hospital elevator smelled like chicken soup. Probably from the food cart that clattered away in front of us. The aroma made my mouth water. I clutched the paper sack stuffed with cookies tighter in my fist, fighting the hunger. Mom would want these cookies. She loved chocolate chip cookies. She used to make us chocolate chip cookies.

The elevator filled with people, and the doors closed. Karen pressed the button for the sixth floor. The panel above it read 6TH FLOOR, PSYCHIATRIC. I shrank back, hoping no one noticed that Karen and I were together.

Thankfully, we were the only ones left on the elevator by the time it reached the top floor. The elevator doors opened to a glassed-in nurses’ station. Now all I smelled was that sick hospital odor.

On each side of the station, signs over locked steel doors said AUTHORIZED PERSONNEL ONLY. Which we weren’t.

Karen approached the window. A nurse glanced up and smiled. “May I help you?” She spoke through a circle in the glass.

“We’d like to visit Patrice Dillon.”

“Are you family?” she asked.

“This is her daughter. I’m the children’s social worker.”

I tried to look invisible.

The nurse slid open a panel under the hole. “Sign in, please.”

After Karen signed our names, the nurse got up and unlocked the door. Inside the ward, it felt eerie. The nurse asked us to follow her. At the first room someone peered out through a small reinforced-glass window. The door rattled and the woman yelled a muffled curse. A man sobbed audibly in the next room. My first thought was, Thank God Michael didn't come. He'd be so freaked.

"Wait here in the community room," the nurse told us. "I'll bring Mrs. Dillon down."

There were several other people in the room. All patients, I assumed. One of them, a man with greasy hair, leered at me. It made me move closer to Karen. An old lady smiled. Rotten teeth.

I trailed Karen to the far corner where an empty easy chair adjoined a loveseat. We both sat on the loveseat. Karen patted my knee. "You okay?"

I clutched the cookies. "Fine."

"It's not what you expected, is it?"

I shrugged. What did I expect?

She said, "I think it's rather homey."

What home did *you* escape from? I almost said.

The nurse reappeared. "Here we are."

Karen and I stood. Mom sat slumped in a wheelchair, her hair all ratty. She wore a green hospital gown and her flowered slippers. How'd she get her slippers? I wondered. "Mom?" I crouched down in front of her.

Her head rose slightly and she smiled. "Antonia? My sweet baby girl?" Her voice sounded hollow.

Tears choked me. "So"—I swallowed them down—"how are you feeling?"

I saw the nurse flash ten fingers at Karen. We didn't have much time. "I brought you a present," I told Mom. Setting the sack in her lap, I added, "Cookies. Your favorite, chocolate chip."

"Mmmm." Mom smiled.

She looked tired. Tired and beaten. The bags under her eyes were puffy and dark. "Antonia," she said again. "My sweet baby girl."

I wanted to shake her. I wanted to shake her and shake her until she woke up. Until she was normal again. Until she was Mom again.

I turned to Karen. "We have to go now, right?"

Karen blinked and nodded. "Right," she said. "Mrs. Dillon, get well soon. Don't worry about the kids. There are some very nice people looking after them for you."

Mom smiled again. "Thank you," she whispered. She looked at me, then down at the cookies. Her hands were trembling. Suddenly she dissolved into tears and crushed the cookies to her face.

The nurse, who'd been standing by, rushed over and wheeled her around. "I'm sorry," the nurse said. "She's having a rough day."

When Mom was gone, I whirled on Karen. "I thought you said she was better. You said she wanted to see us."

"She did." Karen reached for me and I lurched back. "I'm sorry, Antonia."

Everybody's sorry. Sorry, sorry, sorry. Back at the elevator I stood punching the button. Why didn't it come? Why? Finally the doors opened. In silence we rode down. And out. I just wanted out.

We didn't talk at all until we strapped on our seat belts and Karen backed out of the parking space. She said, "The doctor told me she was ready for a family visit."

"A family visit? She didn't even ask about Michael and Chuckie. I bet she doesn't even remember them. She barely remembered me." All of it, all my anger, all my fear and fatigue, my hurt and humiliation, it all poured out at Karen.

"It'll take a while for her medication to take effect," she said calmly.

"Medication!" I nearly screamed. "What kind of medication? She's doped up like a zombie. She isn't any better. If anything, she's worse."

"It sometimes takes up to six weeks before you see any improvement." She turned to me. "She will improve, Antonia. I promise."

"Yeah, right." What did a promise from her mean? "They're frying her brain with drugs," I mumbled.

Karen sighed. "That's how it seems at first," she said. "But the doctors will find the best drug for her and the right dose. It takes time. You wait. In a couple of months, you won't recognize her."

"I don't recognize her now."

Karen looked away. I inhaled deeply and tried to stop shaking. Tried to quell the eruption inside.

"You want to stop for a burger?" Karen said. "It'll sabotage my diet, but what the hell. Sometimes you just need a Happy Meal. Or three, or six." She smiled somberly.

I didn't think any number of Happy Meals would make me happy. Not ever.

* * *

While we ate our burgers and fries, Karen chattered about her day. She said she had to follow the cops to one house where a divorced dad had kidnapped his kids, then she had to pick up another child from day care when the mother got arrested for dealing drugs.

All I could do was shake my head. "I'd hate your job," I said.

She laughed. "Hey, today was a good day."

I just rolled my eyes and slurped my shake.

"What do you want to be, Antonia?" Karen swirled a fry in our shared pool of ketchup. "Careerwise."

"I don't know." I jabbed my straw in the shake. "Something where I can help people. I thought I wanted to be a doctor, until today." My eyes met Karen's. "What's wrong with my mom?"

Karen wiped her greasy fingers on a napkin and sighed. "She's depressed. Clinically depressed. Do you know what that is?"

"Sort of," I said. I'd been living with it.

"It's a chemical imbalance in the brain. It's a disease. In your mom's case, it's probably a lifelong disease. Has she always been like this?"

"No," I answered. "I mean, yes and no. There were times when she was fine. Happy. Other times she . . . wasn't."

Karen said, "I take it she's been on medication before?"

I nodded. I never really knew what the medication was for. "She hates taking pills, though. She said they never worked." I picked up my shake and slurped, then added, "She was right."

Karen replied, "She probably didn't take them long enough to work."

My eyes widened a little.

"It's typical of people like your mom. They don't feel better right away, or they get to feeling better and think they can make it without their medication, so they stop. And the depression just comes back. Worse every time."

I finally asked the question I'd been wanting to. "Is she crazy?"

"No. Oh, no." Karen furrowed her brow. "Not at all. It's a physical condition. It can be controlled with antidepressant drugs and therapy. Just look at me. Do I seem crazy? Don't answer that." She narrowed her eyes.

My eyes about popped out of their sockets. "You're . . . ?"

She spread out her hands, palms up. "Clinically depressed."

"But you act so—so normal."

"Except for my choice of careers, right?" She smiled.

She said it, I didn't. "Doesn't it get to you? Don't you get even more depressed when you see all this ugly stuff every day?"

She shrugged. "Depends on your perspective. I hope I can help. That's a positive thing. It's what keeps me going. Plus, I'm in therapy. But, hey, who isn't?" She chuckled.

Me, I almost said.

Sobering, she added, "Hang in there, kid." She reached across the table and squeezed my hand. "Someday this'll all be a bad dream."

It already is, I thought.

On the way back to the Abeytas' I asked Karen if I could

stop at home and pick up some clothes. Even though Mrs. Luther had bought me a skirt and a couple of tops, I knew I'd run out of things before the end of the week.

"Unfortunately, Antonia, I can't let you go to your house. One of those dumb rules. But if you tell me what you need, I'll stop by and pick it up."

In a way it was a relief not to have to see my house. Not to have to smell the smells, hear the silence, feel the emptiness. "I'll make a list," I told Karen. "And you might want to tell our next-door neighbor, Mrs. Marsh, that we'll be gone for a while." So she doesn't call the cops or have our house condemned, I didn't add.

"We've already talked to her," Karen said. "We've been talking. It's just that we couldn't do anything before."

That made me mad. Mrs. Marsh was such a busybody.

Karen must've seen the scowl on my face because she said, "Mrs. Marsh was worried about you kids, that's all. She's concerned about your mother, too. She took some things over to her in the hospital. And she sent flowers."

My anger dissolved. Why hadn't I thought of that? Mom loved flowers.

Karen added, "Mrs. Marsh said she'd look after your house while you were gone. Oh, and she told me something else sort of interesting. She said you do have a father. She didn't know where he was, but she didn't think he was dead."

Chapter 20

My stomach hurt. At any moment I was going to barf my Big Mac all over Karen's car. Swallowing down the rising bile, I glanced sideways at her.

She didn't accuse me of lying. She just said, "We should tell him what's going on. Do you know where he is?"

"No," I said.

"Okay." She turned back to the road. "We'll try our regular channels."

Don't try too hard, I thought.

Tillie was waiting for us at the door as we pulled in. She opened the screen wide and asked, smiling, "How is she?"

Tillie and Karen exchanged looks. I saw Karen shake her head no. Before Tillie could suffocate me in a hug, I escaped to Yolanda's room.

* * *

I wanted to go back to peer counseling, don't ask me why. Maybe because of what Jazz had said. Even if I didn't give a damn about anything else, I did care about helping her.

Then I remembered, Jazz was staying home the rest of the week to practice. It made the day ahead seem interminable. Until Jazz brushed by me in the hall between first and second periods. "PC," she said without moving her lips.

PC? I glanced over my shoulder at her receding back. Oh, peer counseling. My spirits lifted. I guess she'd decided not to ditch after all.

Jazz was already in her chair when I arrived. "Hey, Tone," she greeted me like nothing had happened.

"Hey." I took my seat. "So, did you finish working on the polonaise?" I pulled out my PC notebook.

"Hell, no," she said. "I'll never get it right. It's my weakest piece. I just can't feel it, you know, here." She slapped her chest. In spite of all her makeup, her face glowed when she talked about her music. The glow extinguished, though, when she added, "Gregoire's going to hate it. And me." Her head fell into her hands. "He'll probably give up on me," she mumbled. "He's the best teacher I've ever had. I'd do anything for Gregoire."

"Anything?"

She lifted her head.

I arched an eyebrow.

"Anything." She added, "Ooh-la-la."

We both cracked up.

I asked, "Are you nervous about competing?"

"No." Jazz scraped nail polish off one thumb. "Yes." She stopped and looked at me. "It's a major competition." She scraped again. "My first one. If I can get a couple of competitions under my belt, I'll have a better chance of being accepted to Juilliard." In a sigh, she said, "It's my dream to go to Juilliard. To be a concert pianist." Her eyes narrowed. "Don't you dare tell anyone. Especially my mother."

I shot an evil grin at her.

She threatened me with a fist. "Did I mention there's a thousand-dollar prize?"

"What!" My eyes popped out.

"But the money doesn't matter. It's the experience that counts."

"Then you can give the money to me," I said.

She snorted. "What would you use it for?"

Without thinking, I replied, "I'd buy my mom some flowers."

Jazz blinked at me. "That's a lot of flowers." She leaned forward on her elbows and said, "Have you seen her? Talked to her?"

Looking away, I mumbled, "Yeah. Last night. Karen took me to the psycho ward."

Jazz opened her mouth.

I held up a hand. "You don't want to know."

"I do if you want to talk about it."

I didn't. I did. Oh, brother. Okay. I started babbling, telling Jazz all about the creepy feeling and the weirdo patients. I told her how my mom was all drugged up and acting like a zombie. "Karen says once the antidepressant takes effect, which could be like weeks or even months, she'll be human again. Karen knows because she's clinically depressed too."

Jazz's jaw unhinged. "Your social worker is a mental case?" She shook her head. "You sure know how to pick 'em."

I glared. "I didn't pick her. And it's not a mental condition, it's physical."

Her eyes softened and she held up two fingers. "Just kidding, Tone. I know that."

My throat caught. Jazz said suddenly, "Let's talk about something else. Could you believe lunch? What was that crap? Ram called it maggot meatloaf."

I chuckled. It reminded me that I'd saved a couple of chocolate chip cookies from my lunch for her. As I handed them over, she stuffed one into her mouth and garbled, "Tone, you're a lifesaver."

The period ended and we stood to leave. "I was going to stay home the next couple of days to practice the putrid polonaise"—Jazz rolled her eyes—"but if you want, I could come for fifth period Friday."

"No, that's okay," I said. "You need all the practice you can get."

"Hey!"

I grinned and left her there, hands on hips. It made me feel warm inside, like maybe peer counseling was important to Jazz. Like maybe I *was* helping her.

* * *

Dr. DiLeo intercepted me on my way out after school. Falling into step beside me in the main hall, he said, "I heard about your mother, Antonia. And the foster home situation. I'm so sorry."

We dodged the boys' track team jogging down the hall toward the gym. "If there's anything I can do . . . If you still want out of the peer counseling program—"

"No," I said quickly. "It's fine. I'm fine."

Dr. DiLeo frowned at me. "You know if you ever need to talk, my door is always open."

Thanks, I thought. You can shut it. I have someone to talk to.

He squeezed my arm and walked away. I wished everyone would stop squeezing me. I might break.

Instead of Luis, Karen was waiting to pick me up after school. Something's happened, I thought. Something bad.

I raced to the car. As I slid in the passenger side and slammed the door, I asked, "Is she all right?"

"Who?" Karen frowned.

"My mom."

"Yes, she's fine. I'm sorry." Karen shook her head. "I didn't mean to scare you."

With a sigh of relief I strapped myself in. As Karen pulled away from the curb, she said, "I got your things."

In the backseat were six or eight grocery bags filled with clothes. "Thanks," I said. "Was the toilet flushed?"

She looked at me funny.

"Never mind." That was stupid.

Karen said, "I think so. It didn't smell."

Good, I thought.

Then she said, "We found your father."

My stomach cramped. Every muscle in my body tensed. When she didn't say anything else, I said it for her. "He's not coming for us, is he."

She exhaled audibly. Sounding mad, she said, "He isn't working right now. He doesn't have any way to support you."

That must've been why the checks stopped coming.

Karen stopped at a red light and turned to face me. "Do you want to talk about it?"

"What's to talk about?" I shrugged. "He left. He isn't coming back. I stopped expecting him to a long time ago." My eyes held Karen's. "Mom's the one who can't deal with it. She still thinks he's going to walk in the door any day now. That everything's going to be back to normal. Maybe you should talk to *her.*"

A horn honked behind us and Karen cursed under her breath. She gunned the motor and tore out. I had to add the last part, didn't I? Now I felt like crying again.

That night, like every other, I shut myself in my room to do homework. Not my room, Yolanda's room. In the middle of recopying my math equations, my pencil broke. "Damn!" I cursed and threw the pencil across the room. Then I just burst into tears. What was wrong with me? I was as bad as Mom.

Which freaked me out. What if I caught her disease? What if I ended up like her?

"This is all your fault," I fumed, staring at the ceiling. "Why did you have to go? You knew how she was. Didn't you care? About her? About us?"

Apparently not, I answered for him. How many times had I been over this? It was useless. My wounds were healed. I didn't even miss him anymore. I wouldn't care at all that he was gone except it left Mom with this gaping hole in her heart. She still loved him; she couldn't let go.

The thought of her locked up in a psycho ward intensified my tears. They just kept coming. They were soaking my math paper and blurring all my answers. Now I'd have to start over—again. Damn!

God, Tone, chill, a voice in my head said.

I took a deep breath.

Finally gaining control, I opened Yolanda's desk to look for another pencil. In a side drawer I noticed a tape recorder. Next to it were a bunch of cassette tapes. Most were old rock groups or Latina singers no one ever heard of. One was this weird-looking Australian band called Sonic Boomerang. How stupid, I thought. I could use a good brain blast, though. I pulled out the recorder and loaded a tape.

Sonic Boomerang wasn't bad. I turned up the volume. At least the noise was numbing enough to get me through my homework.

There was a loud knock on the door. I panicked. Punching the stop button, I thought, Great. I've bothered Tillie and Luis. Now they're going to kick me out. They should, I thought. I've been so ungrateful.

"It's me, Antonia." Michael's voice penetrated the wood.

My heart started again. "Come on in," I said.

"Open the door," he hollered.

Exasperated, I closed my algebra book and wrenched open the door. He stood there, a TV tray grasped in both hands. "Tillie sent you this."

I let him in and told him to set the tray on the desk. There was a plate of cheese and crackers and a can of Dr Pepper. How'd she know I love Dr Pepper? Also on the tray was a little vase with a daisy in it.

Michael said, "She's a real nice lady, huh?"

I glared at him. "Look, don't get comfortable here. As soon as Mom's better we're going home."

"You can," he said.

"Michael!"

"I like it here. I want to stay."

"Sorry, that's not the way it works. We still have parents, Michael. One, anyway," I corrected myself. "We still have a home."

He didn't look convinced. Maybe because I didn't sound convincing.

Michael picked up my hairbrush and ran his index finger along the bristles. "What if Mom doesn't come home?" he said.

"She will. She's better already."

"She's crazy," he said.

"She is not."

"She's crazy and I don't care if I never see her again."

"Michael! She's our mother."

"I don't care. I hate her. I hope she never comes back.

Never. Just like Dad." He flung the hairbrush across the room. Then he raced out, slamming the door behind him.

I shut my eyes and hugged myself. What if he was right? The vision of Mom in the psych ward—I couldn't get it out of my head. It scared me. What *if* she never got better? What if . . .

I banished the thought and wandered over to the window. It was dark out, ink black, with billions of stars blinking overhead. That's how I feel, I thought. Like a star. Not the kind everyone admires and adores. Not the kind with a fan club and a stack of autographed pictures to send out. A star in the sky. Distant. Detached. Blinking. On-off. On-off. It was just me now. Antonia Renee Dillon. No parents. No family. No home.

Chapter 21

I woke up Sunday morning thinking about Jazz. I'd had a dream about her, which was a welcome relief from the nightmares I'd been having about Mom. In the dream Jazz won the Chopin competition and was awarded this giant gold trophy overflowing with money. It made me wonder if she wasn't sending me psychic vibes.

I jumped up and rushed out to the living room. Tillie and Luis were reading the Sunday paper. "Would it be okay if I used the phone?" I asked.

They didn't answer right away, just exchanged uncertain glances.

"It's a local call," I assured them, in case they were worried I might run up their phone bill.

Luis said, "Why don't you use the phone in the den? It'll

be more private." He smiled at Tillie. "Remember how long Yolanda used to talk on that phone? I thought it was going to grow right on to her ear."

Tillie laughed.

"I won't tie it up long," I said.

Tillie said, "You talk as long as you want, honey." She reached out to touch me, but I recoiled. She might think she was Michael's and Chuckie's mom, but she wasn't mine. Yet.

I retrieved Jazz's phone number from my backpack and closed myself in the den. After three rings, Mrs. Luther picked up.

"Hello, Mrs. Luther," I said. "This is Antonia."

"Antonia!" she cried. "How nice to hear from you. How are you, dear?"

"Okay," I lied.

"How are Michael and Chuckie?"

"Good," I said. "Great. Can I talk to Jazz?"

There was a long pause. Mrs. Luther sighed and said, "She can't come to the phone right now." Her voice had changed. She sounded mad. Or sad.

Probably mad. No doubt Jazz was out late celebrating with her friends. She was probably still in bed, dead to the world. "I was just wondering how she did at the piano competition."

Mrs. Luther didn't respond right away. "I'll let her tell you," she finally said. "Have you seen your mother? How is she?"

"Good," I lied again. "Will you tell Jazz I called? Tell her to call me when she gets up?"

“Yes, I will, dear,” she said in another sigh. “You take care. Give your brothers a hug for me.”

“Sure.” I almost added, You’ll have to stand in line.

Jazz never called me back. I hung around downstairs all day waiting. It wasn’t until that night that it struck me. She didn’t have the Abeytas’ phone number. There was probably some stupid rule about giving out foster-home numbers. God, I hated the rules. I hated it here.

The next morning, after Luis dropped me off, I waited for Jazz by the front door. When I spotted her punk groupies rounding the corner of the science wing, I sprinted across the front lawn to catch her. “Hey, Jazz,” I said, out of breath. “How’d you do Saturday?”

She blinked. “Like, what was Saturday?” Her eyes darted nervously from side to side.

Oops. I’d forgotten.

“Hey, it’s someone from the priss patrol,” a guy with spiked hair said. “Quick, shields up.” The other two people crossed their arms in front of their faces.

“You guys,” Jazz said. She yanked down the spiker’s arms.

One of the girls said, “Catch the penny loafers. Those are like so over.”

“Leave her alone,” Jazz sniped. “Come on, let’s go.” She herded the group away. She said something in private and everyone howled. My face flared. Over her shoulder, Jazz held up two fingers. With both hands she spelled out *PC*.

I didn’t acknowledge the message. Just turned and

marched back to the building, trying to swallow down the hurt and humiliation.

Jazz was late. After ten minutes passed, I wondered if I'd misread her message. I wondered if I'd misread Jazz Luther.

The door opened and she dragged in, yanking out a chair and slumping into it. "Don't ask about the competition," she said.

That shut my mouth fast. She must've lost. Mad as I was at her, I never wished her to lose.

"Sorry about this morning." She raised her head. "They didn't mean anything by it. It wasn't personal. Just a game we play with *them.*"

"Them?"

She cocked her head. "You know, the jocks and straights and Jesus freaks."

"You left out prisses."

"And prisses." She dropped her head again.

"I thought you were into respecting everyone's individuality," I said.

She raised her head and glared.

My gaze lowered. I didn't want to fight with her. "I called you Sunday morning to see how you did in the—you know."

"Yeah, I heard." Jazz sat back and dug out her compact. "Just so you know, I'm not allowed to have phone calls. I've been grounded for life."

"Why?" I frowned. "What happened?"

She clicked open the compact and examined her make-up.

"Did it have something to do with the piano competition?"

"Oh, didn't I tell you?" She snapped the compact closed. "I quit the piano."

"Quit?" My jaw bounced off my chest. "You can't quit. Why? How? When did you quit?" I sounded like a blithering idiot.

"In answer to your last question"—she calculated on her fingers—"that would be Friday."

"Before the competition?" My eyes widened. "Why? What happened?" My mind was reeling. Then a vision materialized. The vision of a dress. "Your mom insisted you wear the dress?"

"Bingo." Jazz aimed a lethal fingernail at my face.

"What did Gregoire say? Didn't he—"

"Oh, yeah," she broke in. "I forgot to say, I fired Gregoire. He's a jerk."

I gasped. "Can you do that?"

"What? Call him a jerk?"

I sneered at her. "What happened really?"

She exhaled wearily. Tossing her hair back over her shoulder, she said, "He came over Friday to give me the program; go through the music one more time. This was right after Mom and I got into it about the dress. Mom asked Gregoire what he thought. Like he cares what I wear." She stopped. Her face hardened. "Gregoire said that of course I would have to look presentable. It was expected."

"You mean—"

"That's exactly what I mean," she almost spit at me. "He's a pretentious phony, just like my mother. So I told them if I had to dress all prissy to play in public, I wasn't going to play in public. In fact, I wasn't going to play in private either."

All I could do was gape at her.

A slow smile crept across Jazz's black lips. "You should've seen my father cronk when Mom told him I was quitting the piano." Folding her arms, she slid back in her chair and added, "But I won."

I found my voice. "How do you figure? You didn't play, so you lost the competition."

Her eyes narrowed. "I didn't lose."

"You didn't win," I said.

She opened her mouth to retort when I cut her off. "You don't have to quit the piano over this, do you? I mean, you made your point."

"I hate Gregoire," she muttered.

"So find another teacher. You can't quit, Jazz. You're too good. What about your goal? Your dream to go to Juilliard?"

She cocked her head at me. "That's why they call it a dream, Tone. Because it'll never be a reality."

Chapter 22

Karen came by the Abeytas' that evening to check on us. We were fine, great, according to Tillie and Luis. "Such nice kids, they could stay here forever," Tillie told her. She hugged Chuckie in her lap on the sofa. Next to her, Michael beamed. Next to him, Karen stared at me across the family room. I continued to read my book.

"Antonia, why don't you walk me out?" she said, rising to her feet.

I exhaled loudly and slapped my book closed. Totally rude. Don't ask me why I was taking it out on Karen. Because I was a horrible person, that's why.

When we got to the car, she said, "I stopped by the hospital today. Your mom's looking better. Have you called her?"

I shook my head.

"You can, you know. If you want to go visit again—"

"No," I said sharply. My eyes strayed down the street.

Karen squeezed the stiff hand at my side. "Don't give up hope," she said softly.

Hope, I thought. What was that?

Jazz was right. Any dream I ever had of living a normal life with my own family in our own house was simply that. A dream.

It seemed like the only thing I looked forward to anymore was peer counseling. I hurried to the conference room on Wednesday, late because we had to clean out our lockers during homeroom. Jazz was already there. She didn't even notice me at the door, panting. She had her CD player out, earplugs in, eyes closed. Her fingers tapped on imaginary piano keys across the conference table. That's when it hit me—all those times she'd had her earplugs in, she'd been listening to classical music. Whatever piece she was playing must've ended because she stopped and inhaled deeply.

As I slid into my chair, I clapped and cheered, "Brava!"

Her eyes flew open. She yanked out the earplugs and said, "Sorry. I was just . . ." She started to shove the CD player into her pocket.

"No, wait." I reached over and laid my hand on hers. "What were you playing?"

She shrugged. "It was just the polonaise." Lifting the CD player, she added, "This was a recording Gregoire made of me so I could listen to it at night and visualize." She shook her head. "Putrid polonaise. I had it down perfect by Friday." Her shoulders sagged.

"You're still not playing, are you?"

Jazz dropped the CD player into her pocket. "Tell me more about the abominable Abeytas." She propped her elbows on the table. Her eyes gleamed.

"They're not abominable. They're really nice. Michael and Chuckie love it there. I think Chuckie even stopped wetting the bed."

"What about you?"

"I quit right after I spent the night with you."

She whapped me. "I mean—"

"I know what you mean." I sighed heavily. "It's all right." I stopped. "No, it's not. It feels weird, living there with them. Like we're this make-believe family, in a make-believe house. Just . . . making believe."

"Like Pleasantville," Jazz said.

I frowned at her.

"The movie. Never mind." She waved it off. "So, you feel like an outsider? Like you can't be yourself?"

"Exactly!" I said. "I'm afraid to do anything there. It's not like home, where you can throw your underwear on the floor and no one cares."

Jazz gasped. "You throw your underwear on the floor? My God. Wait till this gets out."

I sneered at her.

She smirked and held up two fingers.

"I know," I said. As an afterthought, I added, "Not that home was all that great. Even before Dad—" I stopped short.

Jazz held my eyes. "Go on," she said.

I shook my head. "Never mind."

"Come on, Tone. Tell me about him. When did he die?"

I swallowed hard.

She added quickly, "You don't have to talk about it. Not if it still hurts. But maybe if you did . . ." She let it dangle.

I bit my lower lip. "He . . . isn't dead."

"What?" She sat bolt upright. "I thought you told me—"

"I never told you that. I said he was gone."

Her eyes darkened. "You knew what I thought."

I opened my mouth to argue, then shut it. She was right. I felt like a worm. "I'm sorry, Jazz. I didn't mean to lie to you. It's just that . . ." I paused. "You know how sometimes a lie gets started and keeps going and going until you start to believe it yourself?" Oh, lame excuse, Antonia.

"Or wish it were true?" Jazz looked at me.

"No!" I frowned at her. "I don't wish my dad was dead. Geez."

Jazz blinked and dropped her head. "I know what you mean about lies," she said. "Sometimes they're even more believable than the truth."

What did she mean by that? Before I could ask, she added, "So what happened with your dad? Why'd he leave?"

"Jazz, I really don't want to talk about him. I don't even want to *think* about him. You know how you figured out Gregoire's a jerk? I figured out my dad's a jerk and a half."

"Are your parents divorced then?"

"Yes. But don't mention it to my mother. She still thinks he's just working late." My eyes welled with tears. I couldn't do this. I had to get out. It was all crashing down. Before I made it to the door, Jazz was there with her arms wrapped around me.

"Don't." I pushed her off.

"I want to help," she said.

"You can't," I almost screeched. "You couldn't possibly understand. Your parents are perfect."

She started to sneer, then stopped. "Tone—"

"I have to clean out my locker," I mumbled, wrenching open the door and hurrying out.

I didn't want to see Jazz on Friday. I wanted to stay home sick. Except I couldn't, since I didn't have a home.

Just as I feared, the session started out the same way as Wednesday's. Jazz was already in the conference room, earplugs in place, fingers flying. This time, though, it was as if she were waiting for me. When I walked through the door, she ripped off the earplugs. But she forgot to turn off the CD player.

I could hear the music. A succession of lilting chords; it sounded like a folk dance.

"The polonaise?" I pointed.

She clicked off the player. "A Bach minuet," she said. "I was going to play it at the recital in May." She smiled, but it seemed forced. She looked different today. Her lipstick had faded to gray. In fact, her whole face looked gray. The same way I felt.

"Jazz," I said, "why don't you just tell your parents you made a mistake. That you were kidding."

"No way." The fire in her eyes reignited. "Then I'd be giving in. I want them to suffer."

"Suffer?" I widened my eyes at her. "Who's suffering?"

"They are," she said. "They're the ones who spent thousands of dollars on my lessons. They bought the baby grand. Without their little piano prodigy, they have absolutely nothing to brag about to their country club phonies."

"Oh, brother." I rolled my eyes. "You think that's all they care about?"

"I know it is."

We locked eyes. Then at the same time we both looked away.

"Parents," Jazz muttered.

"Yeah," I concurred.

A tentative truce passed between us. "I'm sorry about what I said the other day," I began.

"Don't apologize," Jazz said. "I'm sure my parents do seem perfect to you."

"Yeah, well, I don't have to live with them."

"You got that right." She grinned at me. Looking more serious, she added, "I didn't mean to imply that I could ever know how you feel, Tone. I just want you to know, I'm here if you need to talk."

A lump lodged in my throat. I managed a weak nod.

"God." Jazz raked her chipped fingernails through her ratty hair. "This has been the worst week of my life. I am so tense."

"Tell me about it," I said.

She climbed up onto the table and wound into her lotus position. Her index finger beckoned me to follow.

Why not? I thought. It'd be better than baring my soul.

A few minutes into droning our mantras, I felt surprisingly relaxed. With each "ohmmm" a wave of worry washed away from me. Like waves on sand. I felt as if I were floating. Like that day in the pool when Jazz held me up.

Beside me she said softly, "When did your dad leave?"

The tension returned. But not all of it. I willed myself back to calm. "Three years ago," I answered. "A couple of months after Chuckie was born."

Jazz let out a long "ohmmm." She twisted around to face me.

"Does he call you?"

"No," I said. "Never."

"Do you know where he is?"

I shook my head. "Karen does, I guess. But he's not coming back for us, so who cares?" I closed my eyes and said a silent "ohmmm."

"God," Jazz said. "Did he even say good-bye when he left?"

"Oh, sure." I opened my eyes and turned to face her. "His exact words were, 'I'm leaving, Tone. Promise me you'll look after the boys. Your mother can't. She can't even look after herself.' "

Jazz looked at me. Her eyes were sad. I smiled. "To tell you the truth, I don't miss him. I hardly remember him."

"At all?" Her eyes widened.

"Well, one thing." Closing my eyes and turning away, I said, "He's the only one who ever called me Tone."

Chapter 23

I offered to help Tillie do the laundry Saturday morning, but she told me it was under control. In fact, as I searched around for something to do, I noticed everything was under control. It was weird, having so much time on my hands. I actually felt . . . bored.

Karen dropped by later that afternoon to give us a progress report on Mom. "She has good days and bad days," she told us. We were all gathered around the picnic table out back. Luis played catch with Chuckie while Michael squirmed at my side, itching to go play with them.

"As soon as there are a whole lot more good days than bad, she'll be coming home." Karen smiled at Michael. His eyes darted back to Luis and Chuckie. In a lowered voice,

Karen said to Tillie and me, "The doctors are still working on finding the right antidepressant for her. She's experiencing some severe side effects and . . ."

I tuned out. The sight of Luis lobbing the ball to Chuckie made me smile. He was so patient with him. Not the way Dad had been with Michael. He used to yell at him if he even dropped the ball. Said he threw like a girl. Suddenly I noticed the silence.

Karen was staring at me. "She'd love for you to call," she said.

"Can I go now?" Michael asked. "I finished my Kool-Aid."

Tillie said, "Go ahead."

Karen said, "Antonia?"

"I will." I pretended exasperation. "I'm just really busy right now, okay?"

She studied my face. Standing to leave, she said, "Whenever you're ready."

At our session on Monday, which had now become a regular meeting time for us, Jazz looked lifeless. She lay slumped over the table, her hair a mass of tangles. Even more than usual. Something else caught my eye. "What's that on your scalp?" I leaned over, squinting for a better look.

She straightened slowly. "It's head art. Ram drew it on in permanent marker. Like it?" She slumped again.

It was the profile of a bald eagle. Fitting, I thought. "Yeah, it's cool," I said. "I bet your parents cronked."

"They didn't care," she mumbled.

Not only did she look like death, she acted it. "You're still holding out, aren't you?"

Her shoulders shrugged.

"Jazz." I touched her arm. "I think they've suffered enough. Don't you?"

She raised her head slowly, as if it were weighed down by lead, and sat up in her seat. Her mascara was smeared. It was obvious she'd been crying.

"Are you okay?" I said.

"Yeah," she replied. "It's just . . ." She shook her head. "My mom and I had a big fight." She rolled her eyes. "So what else is new? She said if I'm not going to play, they're going to sell the piano. *My* piano." Her voice rose. "They have no right." Tears welled in her eyes.

"Jazz, can't you just—"

Her glare cut me short.

"Can't you play when they're not home?"

"That's the problem." She swiped her nose with the back of her hand. "They're always home. At least, *she* is. Couldn't she get a job or something? Check into a psych ward—" Jazz blanched. "Oh, God." She clapped a hand over her mouth. "I'm sorry, Antonia."

"That's okay." I smiled. At least Jazz was back to joking around.

"Have you seen your mom again?" she asked suddenly.

"No." I shook my head. "I can't. I—" Couldn't even say it.

"Can't handle it?" Jazz offered.

I looked at her.

"I know *I* couldn't. All that stuff you told me about the psych—I mean, the hospital. It's giving me bad dreams."

"Me too," I said.

"If it were me," she went on, "I'd be scared shitless to go back there."

"I am! Not just the place—what if she's worse? What if she never gets better? What if we have to live in foster homes the rest of our lives?"

"You won't." Jazz reached out and touched me. "I promise. Everything will work out fine."

"Where have I heard *that* before?" I muttered.

"My mother?"

We both snorted. For some reason, I felt a hundred percent better. "I wish I could help you with your mother."

"Could you dig up some evidence that I was switched at birth?" she said.

I laughed.

She sighed. "You wouldn't happen to have a piano on you."

"Let me check." I searched in my backpack. "Sorry, no."

"Then there isn't anything you can do. There isn't anything anyone can do."

"Maybe I could talk to your mom—"

"No!" Jazz barked. "God, no. This is between me and her. It's my life. I have to be able to do what I want."

"But you're not," I said.

She just looked at me, and slumped over again.

That night as I lay in bed, I couldn't get Jazz out of my mind. The rift between her and her mother had only grown since I'd been counseling her. If that's what I was supposed to help Jazz with, I was a complete and utter failure.

But that didn't bother me as much as how unhappy Jazz was. She'd given up the one thing she loved most in the world. Her music.

Expression meant everything to Jazz. All you had to do was look at her to know that was true. And Jazz's music was the way she expressed the person she was inside — a passionate, strong, joyful person. Whenever I was with her, she made me feel that way. Which, I suddenly realized, was why I liked being around her.

Jazz was also the most stubborn person I'd ever met. Or proudest. She'd never give in to her mother now. She couldn't.

Lying on Yolanda's bed, staring at a greased-up guy on a poster, I wished there were some way I could get Jazz playing again. Some way to bring her music back to her.

You wouldn't happen to have a piano on you. Jazz's plea repeated in my mind.

I shot bolt upright in bed. That was it!

Chapter 24

"Mrs. Thornberg said we could use the piano in here during fifth period," I told Jazz. "There aren't any orchestra or play rehearsals right now." Pulling open the double doors to the school auditorium, I kicked down the doorstop and shoved Jazz in.

She shrank back against the far wall. "I told you I gave up the piano."

"Yeah, I know what you told me." I held up two fingers right in front of her face. "Come on."

I led her down the center aisle to the stage. On the side wall was a panel of light switches, and I flicked them all on. In a blinding flash, the stage illuminated. The whole auditorium lit up.

An old upright piano stood silhouetted against a black backdrop. Jazz wandered over to it. "You think I'm going to play this crappy thing?" She folded her arms in disgust.

"I asked Mrs. Thornberg to order a baby grand for you. It's on the truck."

Jazz sneered.

"Give me a hand," I said. "Let's move it out." I positioned myself behind the monster and pushed. It didn't budge. "Help me!" I ordered her.

She snapped to attention. "Geez, have a hemorrhage." Heaving and grunting, we rolled the beast to center stage. I went back for the piano bench. Shoving it under her rear, I said, "Okay, play."

"I told you—"

I clapped hands over my ears. "I can't hear you."

She met my eyes and held them. I lowered my hands. "You said you had the polonaise down perfect. I don't believe you."

"What?" Her eyes narrowed.

"Prove it," I said.

She frowned at me. But she turned and eyed the keyboard. Lightly she ran her fingers over the keys. A shaky breath escaped her lips.

"Go ahead," I said softly over her shoulder.

She stretched her fingers. Without warning, her hands attacked the keyboard. An explosion of sound erupted from the piano. The music reverberated in the empty auditorium, echoing off the walls, the ceiling, the seats.

Slowly I backed away, down the stairs and off the stage. I slid into a seat in the front row.

Jazz was transformed as she rocked and swayed to the rhythm of her music. Her eyes closed and stayed closed as her fingers pounded up and down the keyboard. Suddenly the music stopped. "Shit," Jazz muttered. "I did it again."

With a determined look on her face, she hit the keys. She played the same passage, then stopped. Her hands fell to her lap and her head lolled backward.

"You're out of practice," I called up to her. "It'll come back."

"It's not that," she said in a small voice. Her head fell forward. She squeezed her eyes shut, as if holding back tears. "I never want to play that polonaise again."

I understood. Even though it was beautiful music, it was painful for her. Associated with bad memories. Sort of like the smell of bacon for me. "Then play the piece you were listening to before. The minuet."

Jazz turned slowly and smiled at me. "The Bach." She raised her fingers over the keys. All at once her hands were dancing, filling the void with music. It was so joyful, so uplifting. A lump lodged in my throat.

What I wouldn't give to have a talent like that. Even a passion. For something. Anything. Like the way I used to feel about gymnastics. Or math. Maybe I had a hidden talent, somewhere down deep. Something I hadn't discovered yet, or let discover me.

The music ended and Jazz sagged forward on the bench. I jumped to my feet, clapping. Behind me, applause echoed down the aisle. Jazz and I both whipped around. Standing in the double doorway were a few people from the front office. Behind them, clapping and whistling, were two of Jazz's punky pals.

Jazz screeched back the bench and shot out of there. "Jazz, wait!" I cried. But she was gone.

I didn't see Jazz the next day and she never showed for our regular Friday peer counseling session. I sat there for twenty-five minutes, then got mad and left. So she hated me for exposing her to her friends. I could understand that. Even though it wasn't my fault. Is that what she thought? That I'd arranged for those guys to be there? That I'd tricked her into performing?

It bothered me all afternoon that Jazz might think I'd set her up. I couldn't even finish my lasagna at dinner. "Are you all right, Antonia?" Luis asked. "Last time Tillie made lasagna, you ate like a horse."

"I guess I'm just not hungry. It's delicious, though." I didn't want to hurt Tillie's feelings. "Maybe you could save it for me. May I please be excused?"

Tillie said, "Sure. I'll put your dinner in the fridge, in case you want a midnight snack." She smiled.

I forced a smile back. At the door I twisted around. "Would it be all right if I used your phone again? I won't talk long."

Tillie flapped a hand at me. "Gab as long as you—"

I raced to the den and dialed Jazz's number. It rang once, twice. "Hello?" a man answered.

It startled me. "Uh, hello, Mr. Luther? Is Jazz there?"

"Who's this?"

"It's Antonia Dillon." My voice cracked.

"Antonia, hello," he said, a little less ominously.

I cleared my throat. "I know Jazz is grounded, but I really need to talk to her. It'll just take a minute."

He hesitated. "Don't tell Margie, okay? She'll exile me to the guest room for a month."

I let out a short laugh. "I won't. I promise."

A few minutes later I heard a click and the faint sound of breathing. "Are you there, Jazz?" Mr. Luther asked.

"No, it's your guilty conscience speaking."

He sighed. "I'm hanging up." Another click sounded.

"So?" Jazz said flatly.

"Listen to me," I said quickly. "I didn't plan for those guys to be there in the auditorium. They must've seen the crowd or heard you playing and come in to listen."

She didn't respond. In the background heavy metal music blasted away. "Just a minute," Jazz said. The volume lowered and she came back on. "God, that piano is so out of tune. I sounded awful."

"Awful? You were awesome."

"Yeah, right," she muttered.

"Didn't you hear them clapping? They loved it. They thought you were fantastic."

"They were whistling. They thought I was a geek," she said.

"They know better. Don't they?"

She snorted. In a smaller voice, she said, "I feel so guilty, like a criminal. They keep asking me why I'm in such a bad mood and I can't tell them. They know I'm hiding something. They think I don't trust them."

"I don't see why you can't tell them. What kinds of friends are they if they can't accept the real you?"

I guess she didn't have an answer for that. After a long silence, she said, "That piano hasn't been tuned since it was made. Middle C sticks. The pedals don't work. Good thing Bach's dead. If he heard me play his Minuet in G like that, he'd have killed himself."

So that was it. Besides her secret being revealed, she was afraid her performance had been less than perfect. I understood. It was the same way I felt about homework assignments. They had to be perfect. Not that I felt a passion for homework; that'd be stupid.

"I wouldn't worry too much about the piano," I told her. "They were all watching you. Believe me, you were sensational."

"They weren't supposed to be watching me," she snarled. "They were supposed to be experiencing the music."

"They were. At least I was. Everyone else might've been surprised to see who was playing it. No offense."

She didn't say anything.

"Jazz, I didn't mean—"

"I know what you meant," she broke in. After a slight hesitation, she said softly, "Can we do it again Monday? After we talk?"

"That was the plan," I said.

"Uh-oh. I just heard my mom on the stairs. I better go. Tone? I mean, Antonia?"

"Yeah?"

"Thank you," she said, and hung up.

Chapter 25

From the end of the hall I could see Jazz standing outside the conference room door, stretching her fingers and shaking out her hands.

"Jazz," I called to her. "Let's just go to the auditorium. We don't need to talk today."

She rushed up to me. "Are you sure?" The color had returned to her face and her eyes gleamed again. She was psyched.

So was I. "Yes, I'm sure. Come on." I had my reason for not wanting to meet officially, but she didn't need to know.

At the auditorium door Jazz blocked my entrance. "I have to tell you something, Tone. Antonia. Geez!" She smacked her own head. "I keep thinking about this and"

—holding my eyes, she finished—"I think what your dad did really stinks. Abandoning you guys like that. Ram's dad's a bastard, too, but at least he calls once in a while."

My face flared. "You told Ram about my dad?"

Jazz's jaw dropped. "Of course not. That'd break the oath of confidentiality. Not to mention, I might get fired."

"From what?"

Jazz opened her mouth to answer, then shut it. A couple of teachers emerged from the copy room and headed our way. "Oops." Jazz yanked open the door and shoved me in. "You don't want to get a bad rep for hanging with me."

I clucked. Brushing by her, I said, "I can hang with anyone I want."

"Ooh." Jazz widened her eyes. She made sure to shut the door behind us. "Look out, world. I've created a monster."

I twisted around. "Maybe I already was one. Like you said, bad and bode."

Jazz snorted.

As we scurried down the center aisle, I added, "My dad isn't a bastard. Well, okay, he is. But I can sort of understand why he left. He just couldn't take it anymore."

"Couldn't take what?" We'd reached the stage and I flicked on the lights. Jazz didn't race to the piano, the way I expected. She stalled at the bottom of the stairs, waiting for me to answer.

"Mom," I said. "And us, too." My hollow voice echoed in the closed hall. "Go on." I waved her off. "We don't have that much time."

She didn't move. "Maybe we should talk today."

"We'll talk Wednesday. Now go. Dazzle me with your brilliance."

She took the stairs two at a time. As I resumed my seat in front, I called up to her, "What are you going to play?"

"I don't know." She scraped back the bench. "I was going to sneak out some sheet music this morning, but Mom was hanging around the piano. I don't know what she was doing; she can't even play 'Chopsticks.' She was just sitting on the bench, staring. Probably at her own reflection. Anyway, the only things I have totally memorized are the Chopin and the pieces I was going to play for my recital."

"Play what you were going to play for the recital," I said.

While Jazz played, I worked on my homework. The live music was better background than any tape or CD. We were both so absorbed in what we were doing that when the bell rang we shrieked in unison. Gathering my things, I followed Jazz to the restroom. Even though it'd make me late, I *had* to go.

When I came out of the stall, Jazz was standing at the mirror. She offered me her black lipstick. I declined. She said, "What happened to bad and bode?"

I sneered at her and left.

Wednesday, when I arrived at the conference room, Jazz was perched on the table, tucked into her lotus position. Her eyes were closed, thumbs and index fingers pressed together. "Ohmmm," she droned.

It made me happy to see her back to her old self. I shut the door behind me and considered joining her. She seemed deep in her meditation, though, so I slipped quietly into my chair.

"Bode," Jazz droned. "And baaad," she bleated like a sheep.

"Shut up," I said.

"You take everything so personally." She stuck out her tongue stud. "It's just my new mantra. Bode," she droned.

By habit, I reached down for my peer counseling folder, then thought, Oh, forget it. We'd pretty much blown the program.

Jazz slid off the table and looped a leg over her chair catty-corner from me. She crossed her arms on the table and rested her chin on them. "So talk," she said.

I flinched. "What do you want to know?"

"What did you mean by your dad had enough of you? What were you, like a psycho-punker freak or something?"

I rolled my eyes. "You wish."

She grinned.

I didn't. "It's a lot of responsibility, taking care of two little kids."

"Duh." Jazz sat up. "It's not *your* responsibility."

I looked away.

"Where was your mom?" Jazz asked.

"She was there. Sort of. Do you mind?" I pointed to the tabletop.

Jazz's eyebrows arched. She shot up after me and we both assumed our lotuses, side by side.

"Ohmmm," I said.

"Bode," Jazz said. She peeked over at me.

It made me smile. "After Chuckie was born," I began, "Mom got pretty bad. He was a real cranky baby, which didn't help."

"Is that when your mom got depressed?"

"No. She was always depressed. Ohmmm. Not like . . . what you saw. Ohmmm. But she used to have spells. That's what Dad called them. Sick spells, where she'd have to go to bed for a couple of days. If it lasted longer than that, Dad would start yelling at her, telling her to snap out of it."

"Oh, man. That's cold." Jazz shook her head. "Then one day he just split?"

I nodded.

"And he never called you guys, or wrote, or anything?"

"He might've called Mom. The only thing I ever saw in the mail was the divorce papers. That's when Mom really lost it."

"How long ago was that?" Jazz asked.

I thought back. "Six, seven months." I twisted to face her. "Six, seven years."

"God, Tone. You are so strong. I never could've handled all that."

I blinked away and shrugged. "You do what you have to do. The hardest part is, Mom and I used to be really close. Then she just sort of . . . went away."

"Yeah, I know what you mean," Jazz said. "My mom and I used to be pretty close, too. Then she just sort of . . . became a bitch."

That made me laugh. Sliding off the table, I said, "Come on, let's go to the auditorium."

"It's kinda late now," Jazz said, glancing at her watch.

I peered over her arm. "Already? Wow. Time flies when you're having fun."

She whapped me.

We left together, closing the door behind us. "From now on, let's just meet in the auditorium," I said.

A cloud darkened her face. "I don't want my playing to take the place of our peer counseling."

"It won't," I said. "We can still talk. If you want we could meet every day. We wouldn't have to actually count it—"

"Yo, Jazz," someone called from the end of the hall. "Wait up."

"See you tomorrow." I veered off in the opposite direction.

"Wait." Jazz caught my shirtsleeve.

Her punker pal sauntered up to her. "What's this I hear about the piano? You and snooze music."

"I don't know what you're talking about," Jazz said.

"Eeks told me—"

"Eeks needs to get a life," Jazz cut him off. Changing the subject, she said, "Ram, this is Antonia. Antonia, Ram."

"Hi." I smiled tentatively.

"Hey," he said. In spite of his orange spikes and nose ring, he was kind of cute.

"Don't judge her by her looks," Jazz said to Ram. "Antonia is a good person. The best. A better person than *you'll* ever be."

"Hey!" Even through his war paint, he looked totally offended. "She looks like a babe to me."

Jazz kicked his shin. Spinning him around, she shoved him down the hall. "See ya, Tone," she called over her shoulder.

"Yeah, see ya," Ram said, smiling at me. "I hope."

I floated through the rest of the day.

Chapter 26

"*Prélude à l'après-midi d'un faune,* by Claude Debussy. Translated," Jazz explained, "it means 'prelude to the afternoon of a fawn.' This is my favorite piece in the whole wide world." She lifted her hands over the keys and, with the lightest touch, began to play.

Today I just sat back to listen. The music swirled down around me. I could picture it—a fawn following its mother across a mountain meadow. The warm breeze rustling the aspen leaves. I closed my eyes and let the melody sweep me away. So calming, so comforting.

Then the image changed. It wasn't a fawn, it was me. And it wasn't a doe, but my mother. We were having a picnic. At Cherokee Reservoir. Something I said made her laugh. A deep, resonant laugh that carried in the wind. I couldn't remember the last time my mother laughed like that. The last time she'd been really happy. The last time I'd made her happy.

Suddenly the bubble burst. I wasn't alone. Someone whispered in my ear, "She's amazing."

It was Dr. DiLeo, sitting beside me.

I smiled. "Isn't she?"

He said, "Are you responsible for this?" He motioned to the stage. "Getting her to play?"

My face flared. "No way. She could always play."

"I meant—" He stopped and smiled. We listened through a passage before he turned and whispered, "Is this your peer counseling time?"

"Not really," I said. "I mean, we added some sessions. I felt I needed more time to help Jazz with her problem. One of them, anyway."

"What about you?"

I looked at him. "What do you mean?"

He coughed. "Excuse me." He reached in his pocket and popped a Tic Tac. While he was sucking away, I decided to ask Dr. DiLeo the question I'd been meaning to. The question whose answer I'd been dreading. "When are Jazz's fifteen hours up?"

"Her fifteen hours?" He looked confused.

Someone else slid in on the other side of me. "Hello, Antonia," Mrs. Bartoli whispered. "Who is that?" She motioned up to the stage.

"It's Jazz." I twisted to face her. "Jazz Luther."

Her eyes bulged. She dug her glasses out of her blazer pocket and shoved them on.

I added, "She's incredible, isn't she?"

Mrs. Bartoli didn't answer, just sat and stared. I loved her reaction. The shock, the disbelief. Jazz would love it, too, when I told her. If I told her.

"You look surprised," I said to Mrs. Bartoli.

"Well, I . . ." She blinked at me and shook her head. "I just never knew she was so talented."

"Oh, yeah," I said. "She's talented in lots of ways. Like she's really, really smart. She gets straight A's, almost."

"No," Mrs. Bartoli said. "Jazz?" She gawked up at the stage.

"I know," I babbled on, "it's hard to get past her looks, but deep down, she's a really cool person."

Mrs. Bartoli frowned at me. "Are you two friends?"

I nodded. "Good friends." I didn't know if that was true, but I felt close to Jazz. We'd been through a lot together.

Mrs. Bartoli seemed a little shaken, like she'd had this major revelation. She stayed to listen for a few more minutes, until her watch beeped. When she stood to leave, I told her, "Jazz'll be practicing again tomorrow, if you want to come listen. Oh, Mrs. Bartoli?" I stopped her. "I was thinking about joining math club again. I know it's kind of late in the year, but . . . would that be okay?"

"Of course," she said. A smile curled her lips and her eyes softened. "I'm so glad, Antonia."

The next day, about five minutes into Jazz's performance, I felt another presence occupy the seat next to me. When I saw who it was, I freaked.

"Oh, my God," she breathed. "It's true. She's playing."

Oh, my God is right, I thought.

Mrs. Luther reached over and clutched my hand. "The Mozart sonata," she said. "Isn't it marvelous? Isn't *she* marvelous? Ohhh . . ." Her hand squeezed mine.

We sat there together, lost in the music. I don't know what she was thinking, but I was imagining this was my mom holding my hand, that we were experiencing a special moment together.

Mrs. Luther sniffled before releasing my hand and unlatching the purse in her lap. She pulled out a lacy hankie. Just as Jazz finished, Mrs. Luther blew her nose.

It caught Jazz's attention. I saw her freeze. Her eyes narrowed before zeroing in on me.

I shrugged, hoping she'd get the message that I had no idea how her mother had found out.

Mrs. Luther stood and applauded wildly. "Brava, brava," she cheered.

Jazz turned away.

Her mother raced up onto the stage. She yanked Jazz up by the shoulders and smothered her in a hug. "Oh, darling. You're playing again. Thank the Lord. Wait until I tell your father." She held Jazz out at arm's length, then pulled her in again.

Jazz stood there like a rag doll, her face expressionless.

Mrs. Luther said, "You *are* going to play in that recital."

Jazz pushed her back. "No, Mother. I'm *not.*"

"Yes, you are."

They stood eye to eye. A bolt of lightning couldn't cut through the tension. Then a tear rolled down Mrs. Luther's face. "I don't give a damn what you wear," she said. "You are *going* to play." She pulled Jazz in close again. "Oh, darling. Seeing you play again makes me so happy."

Jazz's hands lifted to spread across her mother's back. A slow smile of victory spread across Jazz's face.

My eyes welled with tears. I had to get out of there fast.

Saturday morning Tillie and Luis had planned to take us to Six Flags, but I begged off with a headache. "Would you like me to stay home with you?" Tillie asked, reaching up to feel my forehead.

I recoiled. "No, I'll be fine. I think I'm just tired."

She smiled sympathetically. "If you get hungry, there are lots of leftovers in the fridge. The cookie can is full, too, so help yourself. Don't be a stranger."

A strange thing to say to a stranger, I thought.

After they left, it took me an hour to work up the courage. Three times I picked up the phone and dialed. As soon as it rang, I hung up. I was so afraid.

"Afraid of what?" I asked myself aloud. "She's your mother."

On the fourth try, a receptionist answered. When I asked to speak to Patrice Dillon, the lady said, "Just a moment." It was a long moment before someone else said, "Psychiatric. This is Nancy. Can I help you?"

"May I please speak to Patrice Dillon?" My voice sounded strained, far away.

"Who may I say is calling?"

"Her daughter." I swallowed hard.

She hesitated. "Hang on."

This was my chance. I could hang up now and forget it.

But what if the nurse told Mom I was on the phone and when she answered I wasn't there? It might make her sad. Might cause a relapse. Even worse, what if she was so drugged up she didn't remember she had a daughter?

"Antonia?"

Her voice washed out my worries. "Mom?"

"Antonia, sweetheart. How are you? I'm so happy to hear your voice. How are you? What are you doing? Where are you?"

I chuckled. "I'm fine, Mom. I'm here, at the Abey—the foster home." It might be against the rules to reveal their identity. Oh, so what? "The Abeytas'," I said. "Tillie and Luis."

"Where are Michael and Chuckie? Are they there with you?"

She remembered them. I breathed a sigh of relief. "No, they all went to Six Flags."

"You didn't go?"

"I wanted to talk to you. You know, in private."

"Oh, sweetheart." She sighed, long and loud.

"How are you, Mom?" I asked.

"Much, much better," she answered.

"Really?"

"Really. I think I'll be coming home soon."

"When?"

"I don't know exactly. The doctor said he'd like me to stay at least another week. Just to be sure . . ." She paused. "I think it's a good idea. To be sure."

"Me too," I said. Oh, please be sure in a week, I prayed.

We talked for a long time. She asked about me and

school and the boys. What the foster home was like. I told her it was okay, but not as good as home. That the Abeytas were nice, but not as nice as her. I think that made her happy.

"Boy," Mom said, "the food here sure stinks. First thing I'm going to do when I get sprung is order a bucket of KFC, extra spicy, extra crispy. After I hug you guys to death."

I giggled and said, "If we don't hug you to death first."

Chapter 27

By my calculation the fifteen hours were up. Had been since last week. More than anything in the world I wanted to see Jazz on Monday. To tell her the news. I raced to the auditorium straight from fourth period, hoping, praying she'd be there. That she'd lost track. That she'd show up to play, at least. When I rounded the corner and caught a glimpse of pink hair, I let out a silent cheer.

Jazz lounged against the door, picking at her nail polish. "Come on," I said, grabbing the door handles. "I have so much to tell you."

She widened her eyes at me. "Did you get a tattoo or something? You're, like, glowing."

I sneered at her.

She pushed the door shut against my tug. "We don't

have to meet here anymore," she said. "I get to play a real piano again. My own." She grinned.

My heart plunged. Until she added, "So let's go back to the conference room, where it's more private."

I grabbed her wrist and ran. As soon as the door closed behind us, I blurted, "I talked to my mom this weekend. She says she'll be getting out of the hospital soon."

Jazz gasped. "That is so great. Then you can all go home." She smothered me in a hug.

"Yeah."

She released me and met my eyes. "What? You don't want to go?"

"Of course I do," I said. "It's what I want most in the world. But—"

"You're still scared?"

How'd she know? "A little. A lot. What if it's like before?"

"It won't be. Your mom's better. Isn't she?"

"Lots," I said. "And she doesn't want to leave until she's totally well."

"Then she will be." Jazz squeezed my arms. "You'll have your family back. That's what's important. You'll all be together again."

Taking my chair, I scoffed and said, "If I can drag Michael away from the Abeytas." I told her how he didn't even want to talk about Mom. How he'd totally forgotten her.

"He doesn't understand about family," Jazz said. "How you only really have one true family and you have to love them no matter what. Unconditionally."

An ironic statement coming from her.

She added, "Your brother's seen a lot of bad things go down. Maybe he could use some counseling."

"Yeah, maybe."

"I mean, it seems to have helped you." She cocked her head.

I blinked. "What do you mean?"

Jazz's face paled ghost-white against her black lipstick. Without warning, she leapt up onto the table and assumed her lotus. "Hey, I heard you were going to join math club again."

"Where'd you hear that?"

"I . . ." Her eyes darted around. "I'm not sure. Someone told me."

Nobody knew except Mrs. Bartoli. And I didn't think *she'd* confided in Jazz. "What's going on, Jazz? How do you know stuff about me I've never told you? Are you spying on me?"

"No! Of course not." She crossed her arms over her chest. "I . . ." Her arms dropped. She seemed to be struck speechless. Which was unusual for Jazz Luther. She slid off the table and stood before me. "I can't do this anymore. It's so bogus." She reached out and grasped the doorknob. "We'd better find DiLeo," she said. "There's something you need to know."

Oh, God, I thought. Here it comes.

"I didn't want to deceive you," Jazz said, hopping up onto Dr. DiLeo's desk. "Honest. I was going to tell you—"

What was she talking about?

Dr. DiLeo motioned me to sit. "The whole setup was my idea," he said. "I didn't think you'd agree to counseling if I told you the truth, Antonia."

What was *he* talking about? My mind was reeling. "The truth being?" I asked. I shifted in the steel chair to face both of them. Jazz swung her legs over the edge of his desk while Dr. DiLeo moved around behind her, wedging a shoulder against the filing cabinet.

He held my eyes. "That your family situation was deteriorating and people were concerned about you."

"Who? What people?"

"Mrs. Bartoli, for one. Your neighbor Mrs. Marsh. They both felt you were in trouble. That someone needed to intervene."

My face flared. I hated the thought of people talking about me behind my back.

Dr. DiLeo said, "I paired you up with Jazz because I thought you could help each other."

"What?" Jazz whirled on him.

"Now, don't get mad," he said, holding up his hands. "I know you've been having some family problems of your own, Jazz. Your mother called me a couple of months ago—"

"My mother!"

"And after you quit the piano, she threatened me with . . . well, we won't go there." He focused on me. "So you really *were* acting as a peer counselor, Antonia." He ignored the fire shooting out of Jazz's eyes. Smiling, he added, "That wasn't a lie."

I don't know which of us was angrier. Me, I'd bet, even though Jazz was the first to storm out. My departure left a trail of smoke in its wake.

"Jerk," she muttered, slamming a fist into the nearest locker. "He thinks *I* need counseling?"

I could barely look at her. "You tricked me," I said.

"It wasn't like that—"

"You knew everything about me before we even started."

"No," she snapped. "No. All he told me was that you were having family problems. I guess he thought I'd understand." Her eyes narrowed.

"You knew about my mom. What was going on."

"No!" she yelled. In a calmer voice, she added, "I didn't. Not until you told me. Look, Tone. Antonia! God! I'm really sorry I wasn't honest with you right off. I wanted to tell you, I really did. Especially after you came to my house and everything. But DiLeo made me promise." She torched his office with her eyes.

"And the fifteen hours? That was just—"

"A story I made up," she said. "So you'd buy into this crap."

Which I had. My vision blurred. I whirled around and walked away. I heard Jazz charge off in the opposite direction. I didn't know about her, but I felt so hurt and humiliated I just wanted to crawl in a hole and die.

Chapter 28

Since I didn't have peer counseling to look forward to anymore, I had a lot of time to look back. The assignment was over, that was for sure. Forget my responsibility. Forget my commitment. Forget Jazz Luther. For the next week, though, every time I passed our conference room on my way to history, a claw reached out and pierced my heart.

It wasn't Jazz's fault, I concluded. Okay, yeah, she knew she was counseling me in secret. Sort of an undercover counselor. And it's true that if Dr. DiLeo had been straight with me, I never would've agreed to peer counseling. To *any* counseling. There was nothing wrong with me. At least, I didn't think so.

Except, I did think Jazz helped me. She was someone I

could talk to. In confidence. Someone I trusted. That's what hurt most. She was someone I trusted, but she couldn't trust me enough to tell me the truth.

When I dragged out of school on Friday, Karen was waiting to pick me up. "I have a surprise," she said, smiling.

I tensed. I'd come to dread surprises.

"You're going home tomorrow."

My jaw dropped. "Really?" My whole body went numb. Paralyzed. Can you be paralyzed with joy and fear at the same time?

"She's doing really well, Antonia. You won't even recognize her. What do you say we plan a welcome-home party?"

I bit my lip to stop from crying. All I could do was nod my head.

During dinner, after the Abeytas heard the news that we were leaving, Tillie said, "We could bake a cake for your welcome-home party. And I have some construction paper around here somewhere. Everyone could make a card." She sounded happy, but her eyes looked sad. Especially when they locked on Michael.

Michael hunched over, swirling gravy around in his mashed potatoes.

Chuckie said, "I can write my name."

I jumped up. "Come on, let's do it." I hadn't meant to hurt Tillie's and Luis's feelings, but I think I did. Tillie got up real fast and moved toward the stove. I added quickly, "We really appreciate everything you've done for us. You'll probably be glad to have some peace and quiet around here for a change."

Tillie turned away. Luis smiled somberly. "You're such good kids," he said. "We sure enjoyed having you."

Michael toppled his chair over backward and charged out of the kitchen. Luis and Tillie exchanged looks. Luis sighed and got up to follow Michael.

Tillie gazed longingly out the kitchen door after Michael. No one ever looked at me that way. I hated my brother. I wished he *could* stay here forever.

Karen was coming at noon on Saturday to pick us up. That morning Tillie helped me bake a cake. Mom's favorite—German chocolate. When Karen pulled up, I expected Mom to be in the car, but she wasn't.

"She's waiting for you at the house," Karen explained. "She wanted to get her hair done, clean up a bit, have some time alone at home first."

My expression betrayed my panic. After the last time Mom was left alone . . .

"It's okay, Antonia," Karen said in a lowered voice. "She's all right."

I still couldn't stop shaking inside.

Saying good-bye to the Abeytas was harder than I thought it'd be. Especially for you-know-who. He was stuck to Luis like Velcro. It took both Karen and Tillie to pry him loose.

Twenty minutes later we pulled up to the curb at our house. Karen unstrapped Chuckie and helped him out. Michael just sat there, glowering.

"Well, get out," I said. "Mom's waiting."

"No," he replied. "I don't want to."

"Grow up," I snapped at him. "This is where we live. Not at the Luthers'. Not at the Abeytas'. Here. At the Dillons', 3824 Eaton Street. This is our house, Michael. This is our life. Get used to it."

Michael widened his eyes at me. I guess it sank in because he opened the door and slid out.

"Hello!" Mom called cheerfully from the doorway. She rushed out to meet us.

"Mommy, Mommy, Mommy." Chuckie ran to her.

She wrapped both arms around him and hugged him fiercely. Blinking back tears, she said, "Michael?" She motioned him into the embrace.

He just stood there. I kicked him in the butt, hard.

Mom pulled Michael in. He planted himself like a tree at her feet.

She looked good. Better than she had in a long time. Her hair was cut short and tucked neatly behind her ears. She wore a clean white cotton blouse, which looked freshly ironed, and her black jeans.

Our eyes met and she smiled. She reached across the boys and flicked a tear off my cheek. I didn't even know it was there.

Her eyes strayed to the plate in my hands. "We made you a cake." I offered it to her. "It's your favorite. German chocolate."

She released the boys, took the cake, inhaled deeply, and cocked her head at Michael. "You know how you're always asking, 'Why can't we eat dessert first?' Well, why can't we? Let's go."

We all headed toward the door. Karen pulled me aside

and said, "You call me if she gets bad again, Antonia. Promise."

"I will. I'll make sure she takes her medication."

"No," Karen said. "That's not your responsibility. She needs to make sure she takes her medication and keeps her doctor's appointments. Your neighbor said she'd be glad to drive her, so there's no excuse. It's your mom's job to keep herself well. Also, I'm trying to get her into a support group for women with depression like the one I'm in. But you call me if anything happens before then." She slipped her card into my hand.

It felt good, safe, to know help was a phone call away. "I'll stop in next week to see how you're all doing." She bustled to her car.

"Um, Karen?" I caught up with her at the curb. "Could you maybe see if there's a counselor or something Michael could go to? He's . . . he needs help. Someone to talk to, besides me. All I ever do is get mad at him. I guess I don't understand what he's going through."

Over my head, she frowned at Michael's back. "Yes, I will. I'm glad you said something. I've been so preoccupied with other cases . . . I should've noticed. There are all kinds of resources available. Don't you worry, Antonia. I'll be in touch. You just enjoy being back home with your own family."

She squeezed my shoulder. Instinctively my hand reached up, clamped over hers, and squeezed back.

Chapter 29

Lying face up on my bed, my old lumpy bed—not Yolanda's bed, not Jazz's bed, but my bed—I smiled at the ceiling. The cracked, yellowed ceiling. My ceiling. My walls. My certificates of achievement all thumbtacked in a row. Not a bunch of sweaty strangers staring down at me. This was my room. First thing I did was toss off my shoes. Good. I was home. It felt right.

Wait. Something was different. There was a letter propped against the mirror on my dresser. I got up to check it out. The envelope was addressed to me, but I didn't recognize the writing.

Slipping a thumbnail under the flap, I tore it open and removed the contents. It was a card with my name written on the front: *Ms. Antonia Dillon.*

Imprinted on the inside, in fancy letters, was an invitation:

You are invited to attend
the piano recital of
Jasmine Elizabeth Luther,
Sunday, May 28, at 2:00 P.M.
Bethel Hall

Wow, I thought. She's really going to do it. May 28. That was tomorrow.

Involuntarily my fingers traced across the letters in her name. Did I want to go to her recital?

No.

Yes.

Even though it stung every time I thought about it, our peer counseling sessions had forged a bond between Jazz and me. At least, I felt they had. We'd been avoiding each other, which was no different from before, but I missed Jazz. Since I was the one who'd made it possible for her to practice, to at least have a chance at fulfilling her dream, I really wanted to hear her play.

I sprinted downstairs. "Mom," I said, catching her in the act of hanging up the phone.

"Antonia"—she whirled on me—"you won't believe it. Paul Unger's putting me back on."

"At the salon?

"Yes. It's only part-time to start, but that's okay. I think I need to take it slow."

"That's great, Mom."

She looked so happy. Her face changed suddenly and she said, "It might take a while, but I promise to pay back all your money, Antonia. Every penny." Then she added, "And I'm going to get the rest of our money back, too."

That made *me* happy. "Mom," I started again. "There's this recital I'd like to go to tomorrow."

"Go ahead," she said. "Do you need a ride?"

The thought of making her drive made me tense. "No. I mean, I can take the bus. What I really wanted to ask is if you'd come with me."

She froze. Her eyes glued to my face. She raked fingers through her hair. "I suppose there'll be a lot of people there."

"Probably." Oh, man, what was I doing? "If you don't think you can handle it—"

"No." She cut me off. "Why don't the four of us go? Our whole family."

Our whole family? Had she finally accepted the truth, the reality? I threw my arms around her and squeezed. When she squeezed back, a wall between us crumbled.

A kid in an oversized suit led us to a pew in the back of Bethel Hall. Most of the seats up front were already filled, with a smattering of people in the other pews. My first prayer was that Chuckie could contain himself for two hours. My second prayer was that Mom would make it through.

There were eight pianists on the recital program. All Gregoire's students, I figured out, when he got up to introduce himself and play the opening piece. Jazz played last.

The other students were good. Not as good as Jazz. No way. One student was an old lady who had started playing piano at the age of seventy-two. She wasn't bad, for seventy-two. The other students were younger, more advanced. At least to my untrained ear.

I spotted Mr. and Mrs. Luther sitting in the front pew. They didn't see us. Mrs. Luther was intent on the performance, while Mr. Luther videotaped everyone. I didn't see Ram or any of Jazz's other friends.

After the fourth or fifth piano piece, Chuckie got fidgety, so Mom took him outside. Michael scooted over next to me on the slick seat. "This is boring," he whispered. "When does Jazz play?"

"Soon," I said. I showed him in the program.

Finally it was her turn. I felt anxious, nervous. The anticipation was making me mental. If it was doing that to me, I could imagine how Jazz felt.

What happened next totally blew my mind. This girl, this normal-looking person, strode out onto the stage. It wasn't Jazz. Or if it was, she'd been transformed.

Her hair was brown. A normal-looking shade of brown and it was brushed over the left side and into a knot secured by a pearl barrette. A subtle style that could cover a bald scalp.

She wore a dress. *The* dress. The blue velvet dress with the white ribbon sash, tied in a bow in back. She had on white hose and high heels. Her face showed just a hint of makeup. A little blue eyeshadow, some pink lipstick. No jewelry reflected in the lights—no earrings, no eyebrow rings. No visible tattoos. She smiled timidly.

Mr. Luther moved in with the camcorder to get a better angle. He crouched down in front of the piano. Jazz's eyes swept the audience. I read her expression—sheer terror. Her gaze lit on me and held. Then she took her seat and adjusted the bench.

Jazz closed her eyes. It was so quiet in Bethel Hall, you could've heard the fluttering of angels' wings. Or maybe that was my heart. In a flash, she was off.

Jazz's fingers danced across the keys. I watched as people leaned forward in their pews. There was this collective intake of breath as Jazz flew through the Mozart sonata.

Mom sneaked back with Chuckie. He was dead asleep. He didn't even wake up at the tumultuous applause.

Next Jazz played *Prelude to the Afternoon of a Fawn.* I almost lost it. It was so beautiful, so moving.

All too soon she was finished. She stood to bow and was nearly blown off her feet by the force of applause. Someone yelled, "Brava!" Someone else hollered, "Encore!" People picked up the chant. We all clapped in unison, repeating, "Encore, encore." It woke Chuckie up and he rubbed his eyes. When he joined in the clapping, it made him giggle. Made me giggle. Even Michael smiled.

Jazz sat back down on the piano bench while the audience resumed their seats. Her encore sounded familiar. Only because I'd heard her play it before. The Chopin polonaise.

I closed my eyes and rested my head on Mom's shoulder. I felt this calm, deep sense of something. Joy, maybe. Or hope.

Mom whispered in my ear, "She's wonderful."

"Isn't she?" I beamed. I felt proud, as if Jazz were my creation. She wasn't, of course. She'd sneer at the mere suggestion that she was anyone's creation but her own.

The recital ended and everyone congregated outside. "Antonia, hello!" Mrs. Luther grabbed me in a bear hug. "And Michael and Chuckie." She reached out to touch them both. She enclosed Mom's hand between both of hers. "Mrs. Dillon, Patrice. It's so nice to see you again. I'm Margie Luther, Jasmine's mother."

"Oh, hello," Mom said, smiling. I knew she didn't remember meeting Mrs. Luther. Mrs. Luther knew it, too. "Your daughter plays beautifully," Mom said. "Did you teach her?"

Mrs. Luther laughed. "Not me. I'm tone-deaf as a rock. No, I think she got her musical talent from some long-lost relative. No one in either Laurent's or my family plays any instruments. Our other daughter either. We're all so ordinary next to Jasmine." She glowed.

I wish Jazz could've been there to hear that. To see her mother's face. She'd made her so happy.

Mrs. Luther motioned her husband over and introduced him to Mom. Chuckie gave Mr. Luther a big hug around the legs. Mr. Luther wasn't even embarrassed; he just hugged Chuckie back.

"Here she is now, the prodigal daughter." Mr. Luther turned the camcorder on Jazz.

"Da-ad." She made a face into the lens. She crossed her eyes at me and I laughed.

Mrs. Luther began to tell Mom what lovely manners we all had, what nice children we all were. I wanted to climb out the stained-glass window. Mr. Luther aimed the camcorder at Jazz and me and said, "Okay, you two. You're on. Say something profound for posterity."

"I'll show him my posterity," Jazz muttered and started to turn around.

I caught her arm. "Be nice," I said.

We both faked smiles for the camera.

Jazz said, "Let's get out of here." She grabbed my wrist and yanked me down the front walk.

Chapter 30

We wandered across the lawn and down a hill to a nearby playground. Pausing beside a cluster of purple crocuses, Jazz picked one and said, "I'm glad you came. Got your hair cut; I almost didn't recognize you."

"Me? What about you?"

She held up a hand. "Don't say it. This is the ultimate humiliation, looking like a priss. I don't know how you stand it."

I sneered. "Then why did you do it? Let me guess. To please—"

"You're wrong," she broke in. "Okay, you're right. Can you believe it?" Sticking the crocus behind her ear, she added, "What you said about people watching me and not listening to the music was right, too. I didn't want that to happen. Not today."

"It didn't."

"But don't think I'm sacrificing my temple. Tomorrow it's back to worshiping at my own altar."

"You go, girl," I said.

Jazz howled like a coyote. She peered up the hill to make sure no one, or everyone, was listening.

We both plopped down on swings and began to sway. Jazz pushed off and leaned back. "Hey, your mom looks great," she said in passing.

"Yeah, she's so much better."

"Are you?"

I froze.

Jazz stopped swinging. "Sorry," she said. "Sometimes my mouth—"

"No." I met her eyes. "I am. Thanks to you. You're an awesome peer counselor."

"Yeah, right." She looked away.

"You are," I said. "You really helped me, Jazz. You know you did."

Shaking her head, she murmured, "I wanted to call you so bad, but I didn't think you'd ever want to talk to me again."

"I didn't think you'd want to talk to me."

We both looked down. Jazz said, "I think we need to talk. Especially about what happened."

"Yeah." I ground my shoe in the gravel.

"Because," she went on, "we need to figure out how to

get DiLeo. He deserves a slow, agonizing death. Like rat poison in his Tic Tacs."

I laughed and held up two fingers.

She just seethed.

"We could probably report him," I said. "It's got to be unethical, what he did."

Jazz shook her head. "We better not. They might trash the whole PC program.

"No way," I said.

"Way," she countered.

My eyes widened at her. It was a worthwhile program; a lot of people could use peer counseling. A lot of people like me.

"Seriously, Antonia," Jazz cut into my thoughts. "You really helped me too. My mom and I actually sat down and had a real conversation. About you."

"What?"

"Don't freak," Jazz said. "I didn't tell her anything we talked about in confidence. But it sort of led to this discussion about trust. What it means. And life. What's important to us. Not that anything will change, but we didn't end up screaming at each other. That's something."

That's major, I thought. "You're going to hate me for saying this, Jazz. But I think your mom is a really nice person."

She made a psycho face.

"You're a lot alike. Deep down," I added quickly. "Where it counts."

Jazz turned away. "If you can get past the punk, you mean."

"If you'd let people," I countered.

Jazz twisted around in the swing. "So, have you joined math club yet?" she asked.

"I changed my mind."

She stopped twisting.

"I'm joining swim team instead."

At her shocked expression, I held up two fingers. She snorted and twisted back around in the swing. "Speaking of swimming, next Saturday Mom wants to throw me this big birthday bash." Jazz rolled her eyes. "It's going to be a swim party and she wants me to invite all my friends. Will you come?"

I hesitated. "You really want me to?"

"No, I just told you about it so you'd feel deliberately left out and need long-term psychotherapy." She cocked her head at me. "Yes, I want you to come. According to my father, you're the only *normal* friend I have." She curled a lip. "Plus, Ram's mom is, like, really depressed and drinking again. I thought maybe you could talk to him about it, since you sort of understand what he's going through. If you want to, I mean."

"Yeah, sure. I could do that." A wave of warmth spread through me. I'd *love* to do that. "On one condition," I said.

"What?"

"You play the piano for everyone."

She opened her mouth to object, but I cut her off. "Sink or swim," I said.

She closed her mouth. "I'll think about it," she muttered.

"Think fast. I need to know."

"Geez, have a hemorrhage." Her eyes widened at me. Heaving a heavy sigh, she said, "Yeah, I guess it's time they knew the real geek."

"Jasmine?" Mrs. Luther called down the hill. "Come on, your father wants more movies."

Jazz narrowed her eyes. "I'm going to bust that stupid camcorder over his hundred-dollar haircut."

"No, you're not," I said. "Because you love the attention."

"Antonia," she said, smirking, "you know me too well." She pushed off her swing.

As we started up the hill, I said, "There's something else I wanted to talk to you about, Jazz. I was just kidding before. I am going to join math club."

"You're a glutton for punishment."

"Don't I know it. It's pretty boring with all those nerds, though."

"No doubt. What do you do, recite rational numbers in unison? Or is it verse? 'To be or not to be squared.'"

"Will you shut up a minute?" I whapped her. "What I wanted to ask is, will you join with me?"

She stopped dead. "Math club?"

I arched a hopeful eyebrow.

Her eyes strayed over my shoulder. "God, can you just see Bartoli's face when I walk in with you?"

"She might surprise you. You surprised her." I told Jazz about the afternoon Mrs. Bartoli heard her play. How shocked she was.

Jazz's eyes gleamed. "So, are you thinking what I'm thinking?"

I smiled. "Major ornamentation. Total decoration of the temple. I might have to borrow some clothes, though. All my leather stuff is at the cleaners."

"Antonia," she linked her arm through mine, "you are—"

"Bode," I said. "I know. Bode and bad. I just can't wait to see her cronk."

Define "Normal"
Reading Group Guide

1. Define what you think "normal" means. Is everyone normal? Is normal the best way to be? Is normal the same for everyone? Who gets to decide?

2. Have you ever judged a person on looks, only to find out later that he or she wasn't at all what you expected? Has that changed the way you view people?

3. Whom do you identify most with in the book — Antonia or Jazz? Why?

4. Make a list of the ways in which Antonia and Jazz are alike. Make a list of the ways in which they're different.

5. Freedom of expression is one of the privileges we enjoy in our country, and Jazz has certainly exercised her right. How has her choice to "decorate her temple" affected her goal to become a concert pianist? How has it affected her relationship with her parents? Why do appearance and attitude play such important roles in our lives?

6. After her mother became ill, Antonia chose to isolate herself and deal with the problem on her own. Do you think she made the right decision? What would you have done? Where could Antonia have gone for help?

7. How do you think Antonia and Jazz changed from the beginning of the book to the end? What does this say about the value of friendship?

8. This book has been called contemporary and edgy. What does that mean?

9. Did the story end the way you thought it would? Did your feelings about Antonia and Jazz change? Do you think in real life they could be friends? There's so much discussion these days about acceptance and tolerance of others. Why do you think people have a hard time appreciating and embracing one another's differences?

10. Pretend a year has passed since the events that transpired in *Define "Normal."* What do you imagine has happened to Antonia and Jazz? In other words, what story would you create for the sequel?